Worlds Beyond
My Control

Worlds Beyond My Control

~

A NOVEL

JANE LAZARRE

A DUTTON BOOK

DUTTON
Published by the Penguin Group
Penguin Books USA Inc., 375 Hudson Street, New York, New York 10014, U.S.A.
Penguin Books Ltd, 27 Wrights Lane, London W8 5TZ, England
Penguin Books Australia Ltd, Ringwood, Victoria, Australia
Penguin Books Canada Ltd, 2801 John Street, Markham, Ontario, Canada L3R 1B4
Penguin Books (N.Z.) Ltd, 182-190 Wairau Road, Auckland 10, New Zealand

Penguin Books Ltd, Registered Offices: Harmondsworth, Middlesex, England

First published by Dutton, an imprint of New American Library,
a division of Penguin Books USA Inc.
Distributed in Canada by McClelland & Stewart Inc.

First Printing, April, 1991
10 9 8 7 6 5 4 3 2 1

The lines from "I Stand Here Ironing" by Tillie Olsen, in the collection *Tell Me a
Riddle,* are reprinted by permission from Dell Publishing, a division of Bantam,
Doubleday, Dell Publishing Group, Inc.

 REGISTERED TRADEMARK—MARCA REGISTRADA

LIBRARY OF CONGRESS CATALOGING-IN-PUBLICATION DATA:
Lazarre, Jane.
    Worlds beyond my control : a novel / Jane Lazarre.
      p.   cm.
    I. Title.
    PS3562.A795W6   1991
    813'.54—dc20   90-47452
                                                                         CIP

Printed in the United States of America
Designed by Eve L. Kirch

PUBLISHER'S NOTE
This is a work of fiction. Names, characters, places, and incidents either are
the products of the author's imagination or are used fictitiously, and any re-
semblance to actual persons, living or dead, events, or locales is entirely co-
incidental.

Portions of this book were previously published as follows: "A Slight Distortion of the Truth" was published in *Feminist Studies*; "Shooting Stars" was
published in *VLS*; and "Penetrations" was published in *VLS*.

For Ruth Charney, beloved friend,
and for Simon, Adam, and Khary.

Acknowledgments

I would like to express my gratitude to:

The Yaddo Corporation and to the New York Council on the Arts for a grant and fellowship that enabled me to work on this novel.

The writers who read and comment on everything I write: Miriam Billig, Rebecca Kavaler, Edith Konecky, Carole Rosenthal, and Lynda Schor.

Joyce Engleson, who gave me early encouragement and understanding I will never forget. Also, during a difficult time in publishing, Laurie Bernstein provided unusual attention and sensitivity.

Without the insight and clarity of Gloria Friedman my own consciousness would be fractured, my courage limited.

My debt, both intellectual and emotional, to Sara Ruddick cannot be measured. Without her voice, in person and on the page, I would not know what I know, nor as clearly comprehend what I feel.

My agent and friend, Wendy Weil, is a model of support and loyalty in a rough and callous world. Her assistant, Jennifer Smith, helped in more ways than I can list here.

I don't know if it was for this book in particular, but Denny Hamilton came through.

My family—Douglas White, Adam Lazarre-White, and

Khary Lazarre-White—provided me with love and faith and, perhaps most important to me, trust in my judgment of what aspects of our shared experience I translate into my work.

Finally, the Eugene Lang College of the New School for Social Research blessed me with a sabbatical and a Faculty Development Grant enabling me to finish this novel. I am deeply appreciative of the institution, of the dean of the college, Donald Scott, and especially of my students, whose courage and ideas permeate this book and enrich my life.

To give birth is to create a life that cannot be kept safe, whose unfolding cannot be controlled and whose eventual death is certain. . . . *In a world beyond one's control to be humble is to have a profound sense of the limits of one's actions and of the unpredictability of the consequences of one's work.*

—*Sara Ruddick,* Maternal Thinking:
Toward a Politics of Peace

~ ~ ~

The two strongest foundations of Julia's life are changing so dramatically she fears a structural collapse. She imagines the erosion of a beach taking place slowly, over years. But there is that last day when the sea-change is strong enough to cover the last piece of land. Then, dunes will disappear, homes crumble. Water will turn previously solid signs of human life to crusty, half-identifiable remnants, leagues beneath the surface.

She tries to picture the beach as she walks down Broadway, hassled by beggars whom she alternately gives money to, tries to ignore, hates, fears, then pities so forcefully she may just stop in the crowded street and weep. She sees a woman huddled in a doorway, black skirt shiny with age, and for a dangerous moment she feels she might be that woman next month, next year. She has no reason to believe such a thing. She has a job. A family. Friends. But she has always had trouble maintaining the proper distance. There's always the pit of the crazy, wild, self-flagellating women, suddenly opened beside you, ready to gobble you up.

She said this to Bruce once when he became impatient with her fears and her doubts, the way every ordinary parental concern became an instant obsession with her, especially at three in the morning, when he was trying to sleep. Why are you all this way? he asked her desperately, referring to women. Some days she could name the reasons for him. Other days the opening of the pit is as mysterious to her as to him, to her sons. Suddenly, it is there. She is a wild-woman, devouring things, cursing herself, a monster of self-loathing and need. When her women students describe this state, as they often will in women's literature classes, she tells them she too suffers the madness. No matter how balanced the life, no matter how developed the strength. . . . Her students laugh at her, telling her how strong and transcendent she is. Oh, you think so? She nods at them, knowingly.

She prefers to walk the streets like this, midafternoon, rather than through the park. The solitude of the park frightens her. Remnants of a fearful childhood. But you're not a child anymore, Anthony told her once when he was young—ten, perhaps—and crossing the street she had become startled, as usual, by the mere honking of a horn and, apparently, grabbed his hand so tightly she'd hurt his fingers. You haven't been a child in so long, he'd insisted, rubbing his hands accusingly.

Certain patterns remained. No matter how free she became of old fears (once she could not walk the streets at night; now she found it a pleasure, could decide which streets were safe for wandering after dark; once she heard voices—well, she still hears them, but they no longer frighten her), certain things will happen to her and there she is, back in her child's mind, subject to all sorts of emotional extremity.

Two women pass her, pushing strollers, babies irritable from what must have been a morning in the park. Their faces are sticky with sand and juice; one of them arches in the carriage, shrieking. Tears come to her eyes. Although she remembers clearly the strain of those years, and her own cynicism when older women smiled nostalgically at her children, even if they were in the middle of a temper tantrum, now one of the young women catches her smiling the same nostalgic smile. It's not the babies she wants but the time she felt she could protect them from the world.

The thing about her that most disturbs me, Daniel once told a family therapist, is her anxieties. She was shocked. She had assumed he would say her anger, and this realization was one of the small turning points in the long (interminable, it begins to seem) change she is in. A change of life. It was a phrase with the usual mixture of truth and deceptiveness. She felt shifts dramatic enough to be called life. *But the phrase suggested a definitive moment, something that happened and then was done. No, she thought, jolted into ordinary time by the honking of horns—she was caught in the middle of the street with cars racing toward her—no, it was more like a sea-change, water taking the beach away, over years, until there was nothing left but a narrow strip of hard rock visible only in the lowest tides. For the past few years she'd had a recurring dream that she buried her heart in a cave at the desolate end of a wide white beach. She knelt in the damp dark, digging, patting down mud and sand. Then she walked away from the cave and tried hard to live an admirable life. But part of her was entombed, frozen. "Choose your metaphor," she muttered out loud, and a young black boy, walking past her on the street, stared at her, then looked away, uncomfortable or afraid. Did ordinary white people, obsessed with their own misapprehensions and fears, ever imagine the fear of young black boys?*

She had fallen in love more than twenty years before with Bruce's eyes, his unselfconscious confidence. A young black boy—a young man—two years older than Daniel. When she is out in the world without her family she feels like a woman disguised, one of those Halloween creatures with skin of some otherworldly green. Blacks treat her with short-fused hostility that has become or-

dinary on city streets, on buses, in banks. Whites mur-
mur confessions of racial prejudice, thinking she is one
of them. "Well, every single time I see a sixteen-year-old
black boy, I feel like calling a cop," a woman told her
the other day. She thinks of the sweetness of Anthony's
nature, the softness of his mouth. She feels masked, col-
orless. Or multicolored, some combination outside the
known spectrum with no name to hold her down.

This is her trouble. She cannot keep her mind on one
thing. And the other trouble: she cannot let her children
go gracefully any more than she welcomed them into her
life with ease. Then, at least, she had conviction about
her rights to this and that. Now, she must remain con-
sciously focused (no thoughts about the dangers of the
streets to young black boys, no illusions about hearts
safely entombed) in order to retain for any decent period
her own point of view.

Once, she would have solved the problem by putting it
all into words, as Daniel puts his experience to music,
composing complicated jazz pieces in his old, ragged
black score book from high school. Julia writes descrip-
tions in her journals, thick gray notebooks that pile up
year after year on her shelves. Periodically, she rereads
these records of her emotional life and is amazed at the
repetitions, the way she seems to have to know something
a dozen times before she knows it at all. She also writes
about not writing in her journals. But you do write, her
friends insist. How can you claim to be silent with all
these notebooks?

In her notebooks, Julia is free from the judgment of the
world, but also of the demands of form that define fiction
or memoir. Here, she writes haphazardly, with no atten-
tion to pattern, and that is the trouble. It is pattern she
is after, a form within which someone else might under-
stand. In the perception of convergences of seemingly dis-
tinct experiences lies the only healing she knows. Why
should this be so? Why must she have integration in a

world so marked on its surface by discordance, injustice beyond meaning?

Sounds intrude on her thoughts—police sirens, the longer, more jarring peal of a fire engine, a mother shouting at running children to stop at the corner, an old woman's shuffling gait, close by. She is frightened that she no longer wishes to write to the world. Writing is the only honorable exposure she has been able to imagine in her life, the only place to take off masks and claim a relation. But exposure has become a double-edged sword. Women writers of all ages confess to her their fear of exposure. It's a writing problem, they will say. Yes, but more specifically a woman-writing problem. Just think, she tells her talented friends, of the difference in the idea of exposure in men's and women's history: for women exposure instantly suggests the body, sexuality, badness, shame.

The streets grow unbearably crowded by five o'clock. Subway exits spew out countless numbers of workers, lugging briefcases, shopping bags, children. Teenagers shout at each other from across the street for pages of the math homework. Irritably, people throw some change into a beggar's Styrofoam cup or look at him contemptuously. Julia makes her way through the traffic of people under the weblike constructions that protect pedestrians from the incessant building, renovations of old tenements into expensive co-ops, past the crack dealers who walk among them stealthily until they find the right customer (never her, but she hears their offerings to young men—to Anthony, he told her, every morning on his way to school: Good stuff, man). *Sights and sounds storm through her mind. In recent years, when storms threaten, Julia tends to huddle. Once, she would have met them head on, arms waving, voice loud, descriptive. Now she is wary. She stays inside, keeps the lights on. A strong smell of marijuana wafts around her at the bus stop on the corner, and she looks around to meet the angry eyes of a tall young man in a leather jacket, his head shaved except for a thick stripe across the top. A neighbor walks toward her, a kind man who appears to be seriously ill, pale, leaning on a cane. He smiles warmly at her, and she is frightened he might die soon. She is walking fast now, then she breaks into a jog. When she is finally in her room, she sits still until she is breathing easily again.*

Perhaps she can write as she used to, with simple dec-laration in the first person: I am forty-five years old. I have two sons. *No, not yet. She will have to take the third:* Julia is a woman who writes/a woman who does not write. *Either way (you have to risk it, she has told her students, her own voice smug and hypocritical in her ear) the one who is revealed will be herself.*

ONE

~

A Slight Distortion
of the Truth

~

. . . the maternal task of storytelling . . . a politics of remembering.
 —Maternal Thinking: Toward a
 Politics of Peace, *Sara Ruddick*

It seems to me that in modern prose, the author is duty bound to allow readers to share in the creation of fiction, rather than simply setting it down in front of them as a second reality outside reality.
 —The Fourth Dimension,
 Christa Wolf

A *Slight Distortion* of the Truth

This is a totally autobiographical story which will end up being a distortion of the truth because it is not about me, really. It's about Julia.

This is different from my journal, in which all my voices get mixed up and which is essentially a daily struggle to record life in whatever voice or self is closest to the surface, to work things out, to understand my motivations and needs, to make plans.

It's also different from my real stories, imagined fiction in which I get attached to characters I make up and even dream about. This is different.

This is the actual record of an important experience, but it's not from my point of view. It's from Julia's point of view. And yet, I am going to try to tell the truth.

One of the problems of journal writing is that you have the tendency to complain a lot. The cure will be a form of distancing. I don't have to plow my way through false voices to write this "autobiography." I may not know what I want to say, but I know quite a lot about Julia.

Julia woke up feeling, at first, that she had not slept well. But as soon as she walked into the kitchen where she discovered her older son dressed and eating breakfast,

3

anxious to get to his football practice, she realized she had slept deeply but not well. She must have been tossing and turning all night, trapped in anxiety-filled dreams. She remembered no dreams clearly but was irritated as she poured her coffee because she could sense the trace of one. She was worried that the dream was about Martha and resisted remembering it. If she thought about Martha for one too many minutes, she might go into a rage. Julia didn't want to go into a rage. She wanted to be controlled. She wanted to eat cottage cheese for breakfast, floss her teeth at night, run a mile every day. Lately, Julia loved control. Then suddenly she remembered her dream.

She had been making love to a man she disliked to whom she nevertheless submitted, telling herself that he had the reputation of being a good lover. The point of the dream was that she pretended, successfully, to be attracted to him and greatly aroused. It wasn't that she was afraid of hurting his feelings. But she was unable to act on what she knew to be the truth. She was trapped by a false self, its habits and motivation not her own.

As soon as she remembered the dream, she began badgering Daniel, her son, about money.

"I'm making my lunch, Mom," he said, eager to please. She had criticized him for buying his lunch every day, spending too much. "But I'll need five extra dollars today," he added. "For my gym lock."

"I told you yesterday you wouldn't have enough money for eating out every day," she responded, ignoring his compliance on the lunch question. She was looking for a fight. Next, she criticized her husband, Bruce, for making weak coffee.

Bruce was a man whose capacity for patience was widely known, but his refusal to fight with her was, Julia sometimes felt, a form of contempt.

"I did the best I could," he said, and she was left with a moment of confusion, which turned into anger at Martha. She sipped her coffee and nibbled her toast.

Anthony, Julia's younger son, the person in the family with whom she had the easiest relationship, came out to breakfast. Julia smiled at him. He was the most like herself.

He picked up a half-gallon jug and began pouring milk into his cereal, but he did it carelessly as usual and just missed spilling milk on the table. Julia began to yell at him for what he almost did.

"Okay! Okay!" Anthony shouted.

"Don't say okay to me." Julia grabbed his shoulder and squeezed. Disgusted with herself, she left the room. Her head and back ached. She could think of several reasons why she might be so angry, but none of the reasons sufficed. A dream? The fact that her former best friend didn't want to be friends anymore? Julia could see that might be cause enough for anger, but how could she be angry at someone as stupid as Martha? She dressed for running in spite of the August heat wave, and without saying goodbye to anyone she left the house.

The sun was hot at the reservoir track, and she began very slowly. She looked up at the buildings, blurred gray against the hazy sky. In the evening there was a beautiful light on the buildings, the color of ocean sand, and she could remember last month, sitting at the beach with her other friend Joanie. But she was glad to be running now, not sitting at the beach. She focused on the buildings that encircled the reservoir.

Julia imagines her life surrounded by a brick wall. There is no pathway through the wall, yet she knows she has to pass through it. She has recently completed a novel that has taken her five years to write. The novel is about a woman who loses her sanity because she doesn't believe in the integrity of her own voice. She is made well only when she discovers she has a right to tell her own story, that she is able to find truth from her own point of view. This book, the longest and most complex of any she has

5

written, has been turned down by many publishers. The last two said they couldn't stand the voice of the narrator and main character. She seemed overemotional, too intense, and thoroughly unattractive to them. Julia receives copies of these remarks in the mail with little handwritten notes from her agent: "Don't pay any attention to them," her agent says.

Julia ran the first half mile with ease, and the second half mile was lightened by the shade of the East Side dogwood trees. She missed her running partner, Simone, who was in Paris for the summer visiting her parents, so Julia began talking to herself. She talked about Martha, which was tolerable in a way that thinking about Martha was not.

Martha had come under the influence of a new psychiatrist who convinced her that she had to leave all her intimate friends if she was to grow. Martha, always unable to resist the ideas of men who were attracted to her, as most men were, had decided Julia was one of those people she had to leave.

"Maybe you've already grown big enough," Julia had suggested, looking up at her tall, thin friend.

"It's not a joking matter," Martha had responded, her voice deepening. "I have to be myself. I've never been myself with you. You're too strong and intense."

Julia was amazed. Never herself? They had been friends for over twenty years. Who had she been friends with, Julia wondered, if Martha had never been herself? Maybe the Martha Julia knew was a fictional character. Julia thought that was a good idea for a story she might write. You think you're reading about one person for pages and pages. You get to know that person, to like her. Then all of a sudden you find out you're reading about someone else. She thought it would be a fascinating story, but it would never sell. Readers would get too angry and hate the voice of the narrator.

The night before, Julia had an attack of rage at Martha

6

just when she thought she was about to fall asleep. She woke Bruce up and said, "I'm writing to Martha. I'm going to tell her what I think of her. Why should I let her get away with this?"

"Oh, Jesus," Bruce moaned. "Why? Oh, Christ. Why put yourself in that position? Don't even talk to her. If you see her on the street, say, I don't talk to assholes, and walk on."

Bruce turned over and instantly went back to sleep.

"Martha is not an asshole," Julia objected weakly to his back and shoulders which moved rhythmically with his even breaths. "She was my friend for twenty years."

She felt relieved. She had counted on this reaction from Bruce. She knew it would be madness to try to convince Martha to keep being her friend. She knew she wouldn't do it. Still, she had needed the words in order to extricate the voice that was whispering: *Write to Martha.*

Julia was haunted by false voices, she realized as she made her way to the uptown side of the track, the hardest part of her daily run. But she was so angry, she was running faster than she'd ever gone before. Her back no longer ached. She thought of nothing for the last two minutes except the hot sweat dripping down her neck and between her breasts. At the end of a mile and half she walked down the hill toward the water fountain. "Thank God I forced myself to do this," she muttered as the part of her who decided to run split off from the part who ran.

"I may have an orchestra of voices inside my head, but at least there's one that feels real to me now," Julia said out loud as she walked back to her apartment. She didn't care if people stared at her. She proceeded to converse with herself anyway.

"I have to put Martha behind me," she said. "I must play my parts better." (She pretended to be in an Ingmar Bergman movie she'd seen the week before.)

She entered the elevator, bathed in sweat. Even her earlobes were dripping. "I must do better at the mother role, the worker, the woman nearing forty." She thought this last part, thwarting her need to hear the words spoken, because there were two other people in the elevator.

"I must put on the masks that are right for every situation and see if I can do it without feeling phony. The masks can protect you with distance," she advised herself as the elevator reached her floor.

"Then, when I'm able to do that whenever I want, I will experience . . ."

She stepped out of the elevator.

"Strength and endurance," she said out loud in a very clear voice. The two people on the elevator, hearing her say this, shook their heads. The whole building suspected Julia was crazy.

Julia's problem in life is that she cannot sustain contact with that central, strong self it took her so long to find. Her second problem is that whenever she finds it people accuse her of being too intense. But her biggest problem is that she thinks all the people in the building are constantly thinking about her, wondering if she's crazy. She can't stop imagining she's the center of the universe.

But this fault is also her salvation: she insists on seeing herself as the main character in her story, the narrator of her life. More than anything, in fact, more than breaking down the wall between herself and Bruce, more than Martha's friendship, more than the ocean with Joanie, more even than selling her novel, Julia wants to fuse with that central, sane, and reliable voice she so repeatedly loses. She doesn't believe that life can be expected to provide continual happiness. But Julia wants energy, she wants to remain interested, she wants to feel whole. She no longer believes her fantasies of fame, fortune, and uninterrupted ecstasy. The whole point of writing about myself, Julia, in the third person, as if I (she) were a character in a book, is to try yet another way of using words to strip away my own illusions. I am constantly putting experiences in the

8

wrong categories. I believe my own lies. For instance, I made my friend Martha, who recently ended our friendship, into a character in a story so that I could find some real-sounding voice that would control things. Without that voice, I might have ended up writing her a letter, raging about my pain, begging for her love, believing (astonishingly enough) that if I let her hurt me enough times, she would feel sorry for what she had done and apologize. (As if love were so important that anything at all can be forgiven in its name.) Once Martha becomes a character who has rejected Julia, I can see the pattern clearly—unless of course this so-called story, this skewed autobiography, is really nothing more than a letter to Martha.

Nevertheless, the pattern: a woman whose nature is aloof and self-contained becomes attracted to an intense, overly emotional woman who thrives on intimacy. For years they are good friends, though there is always a push and pull: Martha pulling away, Julia pushing. Julia feels powerful because she possesses her cool friend's love, which is withheld from everyone else. But Martha is haunted by the shadow of her need to remain aloof and self-contained. On the suggestion of a new friend, a man (a psychiatrist), she comes to believe she must reject Julia or lose something crucial to her being. She is happy and strengthened by the decision to end a friendship that is an anachronism in an otherwise smooth and uncontradictory life. Her friend (me) is hurt and angry. However, there is nothing to be done. Martha has her own life to live outside of Julia's story. Whether it is self-betrayal or self-realization is beside the point. She no longer has anything to give the other woman (me), nor anything she wishes to receive. Therefore, the friendship is over.

Julia's son Anthony was friends with Martha's son, Zachary. Julia never approved of the relationship because it was an uncomfortable replica of her friendship with

Martha. Anthony was always calling Zachary for dates, and Zachary was always refusing. Once Julia heard Anthony say to Zachary over the phone, "I really love you, Zachary."

"What did Zachary say when you told him you loved him?" Julia asked when Anthony hung up.

"He didn't say anything," Anthony told her. Then he went to his room and closed the door. Anthony dreamed of himself and Zachary fighting off monsters, robbers, and hurricanes. One of his greatest pleasures was going fishing with Zachary and his father, Martha's husband. The boys would sit in a little boat for hours, unperturbed by the brilliant sun, and wait for a catch. Zachary's father taught them how to clean fish, bread them, and cook them. Both families feasted on the spicy, tender hors d'oeuvres.

"I will never fish with Zachary again," Anthony sobbed as he sat in his bath, right after Julia told him, as gently as she could, that Martha was acting in a way that might cause the friendship between the families to end.

"Zachary has a place in my heart no one else can fill," Anthony moaned, tears cascading down his soft cheeks and forming tiny pools in the crease of his belly.

"Anthony, Anthony, I'm so sorry," Julia soothed, almost crying herself (at his pain, or his writer's use of words?). "I'll tell you what I'll do. . . ."

"There's nothing to do!" he screamed. Daniel rushed in to the bathroom.

"God! What's the matter?!" he said.

"I'm unhappy, that's what's the matter!" Anthony screamed.

Then Bruce came in, so now all four of them were crowded into the tiny bathroom. Julia sat on the rug drenched in bathwater Anthony had angrily slapped out of the tub as he jerked his body around.

"Damn," said Bruce. "Does everything have to be a major drama?"

"With you nothing's a major drama, not even death,"

Julia said, hating herself for her capacity to be mean to Bruce.

"You're so nasty," Daniel criticized his mother in the space left by his father's silence.

"You're right," Julia admitted. "I'm sorry, Bruce," she called to her husband, who had already left the room and didn't respond.

"Doesn't anyone care about me?" Anthony whined.

"What I'll do is this . . ." Julia began as she turned back to her younger son, washing his tan back and neck, running a damp cloth through his large brown curls.

"About what? What's it all about?" demanded Daniel.

"Daniel, please," begged Julia. "Can we finish, please?"

"Okay, okay." Daniel held up his hands as if to stop any further tirade. "Sorry for interfering," he accused his mother with dark, reflective eyes. "But just one thing," he said, turning to the mirror and adjusting his freshly washed hair. "Please can I come home at twelve to-night?" He had just begun going to movies at night, with his friends.

"*No!*" Julia shouted. "Eleven. And that's it. You have to be up at seven. And don't say any more about it." She anticipated trouble.

But he only repeated, his hands up again, keeping her at bay, "Okay, okay, Mom."

She stood up to kiss him good-bye. Though he was only thirteen, her face barely reached his shoulder. She was penetrated by a sharp sorrow. She remembered the fragile infant, the pudgy toddler, the skinny eight-year-old, and all the mistakes she had made.

"What I'll do is this . . ." She turned back to Anthony, who was soaping his hair with shampoo.

But she knew there was nothing she could do—that she could never explain to Anthony or to Daniel what had happened so they would understand, not until they were twenty, or forty, if she lived so long. So on top of this lie, she would have to construct other, smaller lies to her children, those beings to whom she'd once silently sworn she'd never tell an untruth, not after all the distortions of her own childhood, not after so many years of trying to create, or discover, one authentic voice.

"I'll write one last letter to Martha. I'll say how much you would like to see Zachary."

Anthony nodded. "Thanks, Mommy," he whispered.

Julia bent down and hugged him. "I love you," she said. "It will be okay." But she knew it would not be okay, that his was a real sorrow she could do nothing to ease, and that soon, within two or three years, he'd begin to notice. She stood up and stripped off her sopping-wet clothes, wrapped herself in a towel and left the room.

In the kitchen, Bruce was washing dishes.

"Don't you miss them? Don't you feel bad about this? How can we ever come to terms with it?" Julia insisted.

"Yes, I feel very bad, but it's over."

Don't you ever hear false voices seducing you? Julia longed to say. But Bruce would have answered simply, No, I do not. He was so accustomed to her weird questions and to their differences, he didn't even joke about it anymore.

She had written the letter, expecting that at least Martha would answer that, of course, they could work something out, although Julia knew perfectly well there was no way they could work anything out. But Martha had returned a crisp, clear note saying: "I don't want to work anything out. Zachary and Anthony can see each other at baseball practice."

Julia's hands shook with rage when she read the note. "This! After twenty years!" she screamed to the walls. She was unable to cry. She felt the pain move down her like a jet stream, fast, burning, leaving a cool, pleasant emptiness in its wake. The pain, hot and real, lodged behind a rock door. The door was guarded by disembodied voices shouting contradictory instructions to potential intruders, confusing them. Julia no longer cared to battle with the guards. She wanted to be like Bruce. She stood in the kitchen clutching the note, frightened that she was losing something. She wrote down the image of the rock door in her journal.

That afternoon she told Anthony about the note and that there was nothing more to be done. "Okay," he said, and turned back to the newspaper, where he had lately been following the daily sports reports and the wars in the Middle East, discussing both with his father.

"Why are you so calm?" she asked her son. "How come you don't seem upset?"

"Well," he said, looking up from his paper exactly as his father might, "I feel as if something has been dying for a long time and now at last it's dead."

Julia felt stung by the similarity between Anthony and Bruce, but all the boundaries melted with the precision and grace of his language. She nodded respectfully and said no more.

The day Julia went running in the morning to sweat out her anger was two weeks after the note from Martha. She walked around the apartment feeling the end of her long friendship, trying to adjust herself to the shift so that she wouldn't forget suddenly and say to herself, Oh, I'll call Martha and tell her about that. She felt calm rather quickly. Once she would have dived into the pain as if it were a deep natural pond full of secrets, and the courage to dive would have come from her belief in the benefits of feeling to the limit any emotion that registered within her. She looked out the glass door to the small terrace, dusty and sooty from the city air, but nevertheless a corner of beauty she had created. It was crowded with pink and red flowers growing in clay pots of various sizes and long boxes of herbs that, by this time in summer, had gone to seed. She never cut the tiny white flowers from the basil. She liked the lush way they curled and tangled over the sides of the green box. The plants and herbs were bordered by a semicircle of red bricks, leaving clearly demarcated space on the terrace for a chair, a table, a straw mat. Julia felt as if Martha were dead: not recently gone so that her spirit was in every room, but long dead, a distant pleasant memory of a woman Julia had once loved. She felt something inside her filming over, like an animal's eyes when it's drugged. She did not want to split herself into warring feelings, diving into pain: Then she would try to eat herself into wholeness; she might hurt herself by accident with kitchen knives, cutting off the battered part; she knew the pattern well. Once she would have tried to write herself into wholeness. But her novel wouldn't sell.

She went out to the terrace and swept up the dead leaves and grime of the city. She watered the plants, sprayed their leaves until they glistened. She folded Bruce's jogging clothes and laid them on top of a straw basket.

Later that day she decided to walk the thirty blocks to the Y camp to pick up Anthony. Daniel had done the chore for most of the summer, but this week he was at football practice. Thinking about Daniel, she suddenly missed him terribly. Last week they had been together in the apartment all day, hardly talking (she had tried once; he'd refused). He'd played music, read, played Atari. She'd written in her journal. There was a quiet between them in which they could feel the strong love at the bottom of all their conflict. She missed him and was afraid of losing him: she had only five more years to live with him and he would be gone. Then she realized she had been suffering from this future loss ever since he was born.

At Seventy-fifth Street, Julia stopped in a vegetable market. She bought artichokes, the children's favorite, plums, and strawberries. The bag was much heavier than she had anticipated after she had added bread, cheese, cake for dinner, and several days' worth of vegetables. But she decided to walk the remaining ten blocks anyway. On the way, she found herself having a conversation with her sister, who lived in California.

"Why don't you take the bus?" Pamela asked. "It's so hot. And the bag is heavy."

"Oh, I don't mind the strain," Julia answered. "Since I've been running I can tolerate physical pain."

At the wide crosswalk at Sixty-fifth Street, she put down her bag and sighed, stretched her back, and rubbed her aching shoulder. Then she noticed a woman standing next to her. She was a Latina woman of about forty-five wearing a neat blue flowered dress. The woman sighed, too, and placed her bag of vegetables, from the same store as Julia's bag, on the sidewalk while she stretched. Julia smiled and said, "We're both tired for the same reason." The woman laughed and nodded her head.

Across the street, Julia stopped to look in a store window at some shoes. When she started walking again she noticed the Latina woman ahead of her, lugging her bag of vegetables. The woman turned at the same corner Julia was headed for, and they both walked toward the Y. The woman, like Julia, was heading for the camp door, and Julia felt strengthened by this small connection. She is going to pick up her little boy, and she's probably lost a friend, too, Julia thought.

The above incident is actually a distortion. In fact, the Latina woman crossed the street before she reached the Y and headed in a different direction. But this departure from my path filled me with such loneliness that I wanted to change it, and so I made a better ending. I realize now it's only one of many lies I have recorded in this fiction about Julia. For instance, Julia is far more detached here than I really am. Also, I am sure my son was not feeling particularly close to me last week when we spent so much time together. He was, primarily, bored. And I have made Bruce altogether too antithetical to Julia. I love that blunt voice of his that tells the world to fuck off at each rejection. I more than love it. I count on it.

Nevertheless, I stick to my original claim of autobiography. Autobiography is stranger than fiction, which, as everyone knows, must be stranger than life. I never heard from Martha again, and I have not suffered as much as I thought I might. However, I am planning to exaggerate this suffering in my next story about her in order to dramatize the intense connections between women that get pushed behind rock boulders, patrolled by vigilant guards.

The Latina woman, having crossed the street to mail a letter, crossed back over to the side Julia was on, stopped at the door to the camp where she waited for Anthony, and smiled warmly just before a blond, blue-eyed boy rushed out toward her, calling her Inez and declaring his anger at the fact that she had picked him up instead of his mother.

Shooting Stars

Julia walked into the auditorium to see Anthony's school play one evening in late spring and noticed the corded-off front-row seats. She thought at first it was a charming idea. The children were to be made to feel like professional actors, she presumed, for this climax of their third-grade year, this performance for which they had been rehearsing since Christmas. The parents of the cast would be seated in front, their faces proud, self-satisfied, and visible to the children: a source of encouragement. But when she unhooked the rope and proceeded to front row center, she was restrained by a firm hand. It was the hand of Anthony's teacher, Cynthia Springwell, a woman whom Julia had come to dislike despite her assurances, from the beginning of the year, that Anthony was gifted—no, brilliant, the most adorable child Ms. Springwell had ever known.

The previous September Julia had decided to drop by the school to see how Anthony was adjusting to his new class. She thought she would introduce herself to his new teacher in this unannounced, spontaneous way. The teacher was new to the school as well as to Anthony's class, and Julia always liked a teacher to know that her children had what was called an involved mother. These days, teachers were on the lookout for neglected children; mothers who appeared regularly at school were evidence that a child was not psychologically adrift in the world. Any misbehavior, therefore, would be construed as less serious.

On the wall outside room 234, two large oak-tag signs confronted Julia. "Most Popular Girl in the Class," she read. And beneath that: "Handsomest Boy," "Best Athlete," and then "Boy Most Likely to Succeed," and so on through all the categories Julia remembered with a sudden pain in her chest from her own elementary school days. Once she had been voted Prettiest Girl in the Class. But never Most Popular. Sheila Stryzak had always gotten Most Popular. "Prettiest?" her father had scoffed. "Smart is the important thing, Julia. A pretty face is a dime a dozen. Look on the streets if you don't believe me." And he had parted the curtains angrily so Julia could see for herself the meaninglessness, the triviality, of her achievement.

Surely, she hoped, lifting her eyes to the oak-tag once more, in these days of progressive education such competitions were vestigial. Yet here it was, written in red and blue Magic Marker, surrounded by a border of silver stars. Next to Handsomest Boy, Julia read: Anthony Marcus. Her Anthony. And several lines below that, Anthony Marcus again, following Best Athlete. And once more, farther down the list: Most Popular, Anthony Marcus. Julia smiled. Last year, in the second grade, Anthony had trouble every week. She was called in three times by Ms. Goldstein. "Anthony has to learn how to use his mouth instead of his hands," Ms. Goldstein had told her. "He can't ignore anything. A kid teases him—harmless teasing, you know. And right away Anthony is with his fists." Ms. Goldstein held her fists up close to Julia's face, imitating Anthony. Julia retreated from these meetings as if she had been punched.

"Anthony," she would plead with him, "you have to

learn to use your mouth instead of your fists. Why'd you hit Germaine today?"

"He called me a queer," Anthony reported, soft lips curling down into the impending cry that melted Julia's anger like early frost under a strong rain.

"A queer?" she said. "My God, Anthony, what's a queer? Do you even know?"

Anthony wept passionately into his mother's blouse. "It's when you kiss another boy. He saw me kissing Daniel good-bye, and then he said, 'Anthony's a homoselectual, Anthony's a homoselectual.' "

"A *homosexual.*"

"What?" screamed Anthony.

"The word is homosexual, not homoselectual, and little boys aren't homosexuals. Certainly not because they kiss their brothers."

The next day she went back into school to inform Ms. Goldstein that it wasn't Anthony's fault if he had hit some homophobic six-year-old. He was still making an adjustment. But it was true, Anthony couldn't ignore anything. Let anyone hurl an ordinary insult at him in the yard or the lunchroom, make a sign of disgust when peanut butter stuck to his gums where the teeth had fallen out, call him a faggot when he missed the ball, and Anthony would use his fists instead of his mouth.

"Nobody likes me," he'd cry at night. "They think I'm too wild."

And yet here he was: Most Popular. Best Athlete. Handsomest. Even Sheila Stryzak had never achieved more than one category a year.

Then Julia noticed that all but one of the girls' categories were given to the same child—Elinore Ritterman, whom everyone called Ellie. Every single category except Best Athlete, since Ellie was short and frail.

When Julia entered the room, the children were sitting in a circle. Ms. Springwell smiled at her, but Julia signaled that she didn't mean to interrupt. She sat down on one of the small wooden chairs and listened to the circle discussion. Ellie was telling the class about her parents' recent separation.

"My father moved out a few months ago," said Ellie, shifting to her knees, lifting her chin and deepening her voice as if she were on stage. "Now he has a new relationship with a woman. I like Jennifer, but I'm a little jealous." She giggled. All the other children, many of whom had experienced the separation of parents, sat still as grass on a hot day, little heads not moving an inch, mouths slightly opened, lips dry, as Ellie told her tale. Anthony shifted uneasily and looked over at his mother as Ellie continued. "I'm especially upset when I sleep at my Dad's and in the morning I wake up and find Jennifer, sometimes without anything on, in bed with my father. Well," she added after another giggle, "they will be married very soon."

She hadn't paused until she reached the end of her complex sentence. There had been no childish clumsiness, no moment's hesitation among the graceful phrases. Alarmed by this mask of self-possession, Julia was about to offer assistance while Ms. Springwell talked to Ellie in private. But the teacher said, "Thank you, Ellie, for sharing your feelings with us. Here, where there is no one to judge you, you can say anything you want, children. Now who else has parents who've been separated and would like to tell a story to the group?"

When the children went to lunch after circle time, Julia approached Ms. Springwell, hardly knowing where to begin. But Ms. Springwell began before she had the chance to flounder, "Anthony and Ellie are the most brilliant, the most adorable children I've ever met. But Anthony—Anthony's so well adjusted."

"I'm glad to hear it," said Julia. She pulled on her sweatshirt collar and scratched her neck. "Last year he was always getting into trouble."

"Anthony? I can't believe it. He's the best child in the

class. Practically an assistant teacher. I count on him." She dragged on her cigarette, combed dark waves into place. "I mean it. Anthony is a love. You've done a marvelous job with him."

Walking home to get ready for her class that afternoon, Julia wondered if she had failed to question anything she'd seen because she was a coward. No teacher had ever told her she'd done a marvelous job before. Daniel was always berated for talking too much and failing to take direction. "He has a problem with authority," teacher after teacher had said. And then Anthony had shown a propensity for using his fists instead of his mouth. Or, she thought as she gathered her lecture notes, maybe she was still getting back at Sheila Stryzak. She decided it was in Anthony's interest for her to remain silent for the time being. Perhaps he needed this recognition. Only Ellie claimed more categories than Anthony, and Ellie, as everyone had known since kindergarten, was an exceptionally gifted child.

For the next few months Anthony was treated more and more as an assistant in the class. He was Homework Collector and Monitor on the lunch line. Every piece of written work he handed in came back with a large red *A* surrounded by a halo of golden stars. "You've got nine spelling mistakes on this one," Daniel objected one night. "Is your teacher nuts?"

Anthony burst into tears, grabbed his paper, and locked himself in his room. "I think he needs encouragement more than criticism," Julia muttered.

"Encouragement for what?" said Bruce, who was clearing the table with Daniel.

"Recognition," said Julia. "He's finally adjusting to school."

"Recognition for being a shitty speller, and he's adjusting to a world of illusion," said Daniel, who was at least as articulate as Ellie.

When the tenth composition came home in a sunburst

of gold stars surrounding misspelled words and sentence fragments, Julia was converted to Daniel's and Bruce's point of view. Every composition was less thoughtful than the one before. Moreover, Anthony was becoming argumentative and haughty at home. "I can't set the table. I'm feeling depressed," he'd told her the night before. More and more frequently, he had trouble falling asleep.

"What is it?" Julia asked him one night. It was almost midnight, and Anthony's sheets were rumpled into a snakelike cord from his twisting and turning. He had sweat on his face.

"I'm just so hot," he complained.

She straightened his sheets, sang him an old lullaby, her lips drifting over his damp hair. "What's really wrong, Anthony? Are you still having fun at school?"

"The kids don't like me anymore," he told her, nearly in tears. "They say I'm conceited. But don't worry. They hate Ellie more than me."

The following day Julia waited until three o'clock before she went into the school to catch Ms. Springwell for a conference. She had to cancel her class at the college, but her students wouldn't mind. Once, she'd believed that every day she had souls to save, intellectual conversions to which she must attend. But after years of teaching she had learned the more daunting and manageable truth: intellectual conversions were occasional; souls weren't saved every day or even every semester. And furthermore, who was she to save them? It wasn't just that she'd wanted students to come to love literature through her. She had wanted them to need her. And they had come to need her. And some of them had suffered because in the end she couldn't give them what they needed. Now, she kept a greater distance. The distance gave her perspective, and if she had to miss a class, she didn't feel guilty. She felt kind, giving them a free hour.

She would be as direct as possible, Julia swore as she climbed the stairs to the second-floor classroom where she hoped Ms. Springwell would be alone, getting ready to leave for the day. The room was arranged as if it were an artist's loft, divided into areas in the progressive style, no sign of traditional classroom rigidity. Not a desk in sight, thought Julia. "Ms. Springwell?" She touched the woman's arm.

"Oh! Julia. You startled me. Is anything wrong?"

On the walls around the room there were signs instructing the children in methods and goals of psychological health. "Believe in Yourself," Julia read. "You Are a Wonderful Person. Let's Share Feelings."

"Well, not exactly wrong," she said, trying to sound unthreatening. "It's just that Anthony's reacting badly to—his position in the class. He's doing well, I know, and I'm grateful he's so popular." She gestured to the oak-tag signs, now moved into the classroom, on which Anthony had devoured several more categories.

"Oh, he's so popular. And I'm astonished at his brilliance, Julia. You have a gifted child."

"But he's becoming . . ." She paused, not wanting to seem unimpressed by her child's gifts, some domesticated Medea willing to squander his talents for her own needs. "He's, well . . . unrealistic. What they used to call spoiled? He loves the class, I don't mean he doesn't. He likes you."

Cynthia Springwell's rouge darkened slightly over sharp cheekbones.

"And he's not doing too well on his compositions," Julia persisted. "It's not good for kids to be treated like princes and princesses. And Anthony—and, well, if you ask me, Ellie too—they're being given too much attention. Don't the other kids mind that Anthony and Ellie are voted best in everything?"

Cynthia Springwell tied a small silk scarf under her chin. She had come to the school highly recommended by everyone Julia had asked. The principal said she was the best teacher in the entire country. They were lucky to have her. And of course he'd put her right into the gifted class. Smart kids need creative inspiration, he had said.

"I'm not telling you how to teach," Julia added quickly. "But as for Anthony, I would appreciate it if he got a little less special attention. I don't want him made into a star."

The teacher stopped at the doorway, her smile gone. "I know just what you mean. I wasn't aware of the fact that Anthony was getting—as they say—too big for his britches. I'm glad you talked to me, Julia. Don't worry about a thing."

Julia was relieved. The last thing she wanted was an open fight. It was only November, and Anthony had to be in this classroom for eight more months. But by the time she walked several blocks she became aware of her anger. Too big for his britches? She would have to tell Anthony to expect a change.

When she did, Anthony was surprisingly receptive. "Just think," she said, "how you would feel if Germaine or Ronald was voted handsomest, most popular, best athlete, and was boss in almost every activity. Would you like that, Anthony?"

Daniel had been listening at the doorway, and now he said, "Well, if Anthony's really best at everything, what's wrong with saying so?"

"He's not best at everything. No one is," she answered, her attention still focused on Anthony.

"What do you mean, no one is? That's ridiculous."

She tried to think of what she meant.

"Answer me, Mom," Daniel shouted, standing in front of her, blocking her view of Anthony. But with Daniel, her firstborn, that child who had transformed her into a mother, clarity frequently eluded her. She was always sinking into bogs of guilt and self-doubt, earth sucking her in, up to her neck, over her mouth, earth creatures, uncontrollable, slippery, repulsive, settling on her tongue.

"Daniel," she shouted, clutching her anger, hateful tow

rope that always bound her doubly to her unclear words, "stay out of this. Please!"

"Well, all I know is I never acted like he's been acting," Daniel shouted back. "No one around here ever treated me like a prince."

The accuracy of his remark snapped the rope and threw her onto hard ground. Daniel had been a child who was good at nearly everything, forming sentences at two, athletic—teachers called it good hand-eye coordination. But Julia had sworn not to burden her children with a sense of omnipotence that would render them intolerant of failure. For what was possible without the capacity to endure failure? How many artists had been lost? she asked her students, half of whom wanted to be Great Writers, either geniuses or nothing at all. When everyone in the family began to comment on Daniel's many gifts, telling him there had never been a boy like him, Julia had admonished them. I don't want any princes in my house, she had said. But Anthony, younger and slower to develop, seemed to need encouragement. And now here was Daniel, accusing her of neglect. "You're right, Daniel," she said. "He has been acting like a little prince. But it's not his fault, Danny-boy." She used the old pet name, but Daniel lowered black brows at her and she saw premature worry lines appear between his eyes, reflecting her own.

"Did you talk to Anthony?" said Bruce later that night. "Did you talk to that idiot Springwell?"

Julia was too tired to tell him the whole story. "Anthony seems to understand," she said. "I just hope Ms. Springwell doesn't start going to the other extreme, making him feel like a piece of shit."

"Won't hurt him to feel like a piece of shit once in his life. Then he'll have to figure out he's the one who has to know he's not a piece of shit," said Bruce, and the combination of accuracy and convolution in Bruce's emotional logic caused Julia to turn her back to him and close her eyes.

Bruce was never treated like a prince, she thought to herself as she rolled around her side of the bed searching for comfort. Just the opposite. A poor family. No one to exaggerate his talents, to have the confidence or time to notice any. Yet, Bruce was confident. He got things done. He never expected anything to come to him without work. Julia turned back toward her husband and curved around his torso, feeling the hardness of his back. The muscles in his neck, tense from holding his head slightly forward, moved against her cheek. She kissed the tight neck, thought of the determined little boy, and felt pleased by Bruce's successes which she counted as she fell asleep.

Anthony began to behave better at home. His sleeping problems disappeared. Instead of fighting with his family, he was frequently angry at Ms. Springwell. "You should see her," he told Julia one afternoon as he walked in the door, threw his backpack on the floor, raced into the bathroom, and began to pee. "You should see her, Mom," he called. "You should see how she acts."

"Ms. Springwell?"

"No," Anthony said as he walked to the refrigerator, gulped down a swig of juice from the quart, and took a large bite of apple while deciding on an afternoon snack.

"Anthony, don't drink from the quart," Julia said.

"You should see her, Mom. Ellie. She thinks she's the queen. And all the other girls think she's queen, too. But they really hate her. Anyone can tell."

"Remember how hard it was for you, Anthony," Julia cautioned. "It's not all Ellie's fault."

"I know. It's Ms. Springwell's fault. She's totally crazy. You know what she did today? She told us in circle time how she has so many problems with her husband's ex-wife. How the old wife doesn't want the new wife—that's Ms. Springwell—to take care of the kids. She told us all day what a terrible person the old wife was. Is. I mean

26

she's not dead, but I think Ms. Springwell wishes she was."

Julia considered again taking Anthony out of the class. But it was early December. The class had begun preparation for a play to be performed in June. They would rehearse all winter and spring. They would adapt the script themselves. They would make the scenery, perform all over the city, the principal assured them. They would bring all kinds of attention, perhaps in the form of extra funds, to the school. There was no longer any problem with inflated grades on compositions. There were no compositions, nor math or science either. The children were completely involved with the project, and Julia didn't have the heart to separate Anthony from his friends. "Now that I'm regular again, the other kids like me," he reported.

On the day before Christmas vacation, when the children usually brought large shopping bags to carry home their work, Anthony said he wouldn't require a bag this year. "Nothing to bring home," he announced. Indeed, all he brought home was the script for the play. Tryouts were scheduled for the first day after vacation.

"And you know who's the star," Anthony grumbled as he walked in the door that Monday afternoon. "The queen of the world. Only now she thinks she's God."

"You should be able to understand," Daniel told him. "You were acting like a little god all this fall. Remember?"

"Not like her," retorted Anthony. "No one can talk to her anymore. It's not only that she gets all the privileges—like she gets to be the monitor in the yard, and representative on the school court, and she gets chosen to put the chairs on the tables at the end of the day. . . ."

"Put the chairs on the tables? Who wants to do that?" Daniel laughed.

"That's not the point," Anthony yelled. "She gets to do everything. And she thinks she's God." He stomped off to his room, and they heard sobs coming from behind the slammed door.

"He got a shitty part," said Daniel. Bruce rose to go to Anthony, Julia following behind. "He has to learn to handle it," Daniel warned as they departed. "Everyone does."

Daniel had learned to handle it in the fifth grade when his height lagged maddeningly behind his weight. He was chubbier than any of his friends. No amount of athletic valor redeemed him from the apparent sin of this aesthetic failure. "I'm fat," he'd cried in Julia's arms. "You've got to learn how to cope with failure, Mom," he said as she came out of the room, leaving behind a calmer Anthony. But then he contradicted his own sober advice. "Maybe you were wrong to tell Springwell not to give him so much attention. Maybe he would've been better off being a star for once."

"It was having a bad effect on him," Julia murmured, turning on tap water full strength, loudly stacking pots in the sink.

"Well, everyone thinks I'm the greatest in school," said Daniel, reaching over and turning off the water. "Will you listen to me, Mom? Everyone likes me. I'm not saying it's fair, but I'm popular now. And it feels really great. And yo, Mama," he drawled, strutting and sliding across the floor, "I know it's true. I am the greatest!" He opened his arms, a just crowned champion, welcoming applause. A special boy, and despite Julia's prudence for so many years, he had known it all along.

"Do you think you're really special?" Julia asked Bruce as they lay in the dark, Bruce near sleep, Julia coaxing half-formed thoughts into words. "I mean deep down. Do you think you have extraordinary powers?"

"Special?" Bruce mumbled. "Yes, I guess so. In my own way. Extraordinary powers? No, I doubt it." Then he whispered mischievously, "But I know you think you have those powers, Julia. And you do." He nestled his face in her neck, frightening her with his compliance.

"*Thought*," said Julia. "I *thought* I did. I thought everything was possible. It was like believing in magic." Having given up on magic, she practiced competence. A class well planned, an extra mile run around the park, a moment of anger controlled into silence—these achievements had replaced Julia's dreams of glory, books to be written that would change the world, perfect lovers come from nowhere to whisper to her soul. One sort of power always seemed to negate the other, and she shook Bruce, waking him. "Like the way I used to feel about my work? That I could change the world with my words? I don't think that way anymore."

Rehearsals intensified as the school year approached its end. A month remained before opening night, but individual scenes from the play were being performed all over the city. Julia attended several of these performances, each one centered around a song by Ellie Ritterman who had an unusually resonant voice for such a small child. The other children put all their hearts into the short phrases of the backup chorus, tapping their feet to the rhythm of Ellie's solos. After the performance, the girls gathered around her, touching her hair, holding her hand, running admiring fingers down the pleats of her costume, which was far more elaborate than theirs. Julia saw it happen repeatedly—several girls talking to Ellie at once, each competing for her attention, then Ellie lifting her hands to her ears and shouting, "Girls! One at a time!"

Anthony was a butler in the play and had one line in addition to being in the boys' chorus. "Is the laundry ready?" he shouted in the second act, marching aggressively onto the stage and confronting his friend Rhonda, the housekeeper. He practiced the line incessantly, while he bathed, in bed after the light was out, sometimes arriving at dinner with his eyes to the sky, muttering, "Is the laundry ready?'' so that Daniel began telling him, before he had the chance to speak his line, that the laundry was ready so shut the fuck up. Interceding one evening, Bruce asked Anthony why he didn't practice the song for the chorus.

"Ms. Springwell says I can't sing, so I have to kind of whisper the words,'' said Anthony. And it was true, Anthony couldn't carry a tune for more than three notes. Still, Julia felt indignant in his behalf. "How do you like school these days?'' she asked him all through April and May. "Is the rehearsing getting too much for you?''

"No, it's okay,'' Anthony told her. "It's fun. I'm glad I didn't get a big part, though. Ellie gets blamed for everything just 'cause she's the star.''

Two weeks before opening night, Anthony was resentful again. "I can't believe it. I just can't believe what's happening!'' He threw his backpack against the wall, hitting his framed poster of Dr. J., the basketball genius. Glass shattered all over the rug.

"Anthony! For God's sake!'' Julia screamed.

"I can't help it. She gets everything. Last week we had elections for student government, and guess who won by about a million votes? She's the main speaker for school announcements. And now she won the Martin Luther King essay contest. I'm at the end of my rope.''

Julia knelt on green pile, flattened by years of wrestling and Nerf basketball, picking up slivers of glass. "I thought you said nobody liked her anymore,'' she said without conviction. Because she understood: that wouldn't matter. Ellie was on a roll—a star shooting through the school universe, rendering everything dull by comparison.

"They *don't* like her,'' Anthony said, on his knees, too, weeding glass from the matted carpet. He gazed into a large fragment that reflected green rug, blue walls, the dark beige of his finger. "Can I keep this, Mom?'' he asked, momentarily distracted. He held the glass close to his eyes, peering through it at her face.

Julia said, "Yes, if you're careful." She was hypnotized for a moment, with Anthony.

"No one *does* like her," he repeated, placing the glass on his bureau next to his other special things. "But they all want her to like them."

"These two rows are for Ellie's guests," Cynthia Springwell told Julia and Bruce. She pointed to the third row. "There are some empty seats. Right back there."

They retreated obediently and joined the other disgruntled parents, but she was happy to be with them instead of in the first two rows, filled with Ellie's family and friends who smiled intimately at each other and impersonally back at the gathering crowd. The play proceeded with remarkable efficiency. Ms. Springwell was in the wings, issuing directions that were instantly obeyed. Ronald forgot his line once but was punched by an attentive Anthony, who whispered the words in his ear so that the line was delivered only a decibel too loud, only a moment too late. Ellie's presence and command of her part astonished everyone. She belted the songs into the far corners of the auditorium; even the irritated parents of the other children rose to applaud after each one of her solos. She played to the audience yet never stepped outside her part with the giggle the other children occasionally had to suppress.

"You gotta admit, she's good," whispered Daniel. But Julia had gone way beyond admitting that obvious fact. She wept for the power of Ellie's talent, wondering how the child would steer it from here. She broke her building attention to Ellie's every move only to hold her breath while Anthony shouted, *"IS THE LAUNDRY READY?"* so loudly, and with such self-possession, that a number of people clapped for his single line, although Julia suspected Bruce had initiated the applause. Daniel clapped as loudly as anyone but leaned over to whisper, "This applause is because he's a cute kid. Ellie's the real thing, know what I mean, Mom?"

Had she taken something from her child or given him something to get him through? When the curtain came down after the final scene, the audience rose to its feet, shouting bravos. The children filed to the front of the stage, Ellie in the center, Anthony with his hands behind his back, hiding something. The adults clapped for everyone equally. The children in the audience shouted appreciation for Ellie, managed loud whistles: her due. When the crowd quieted down, Anthony stepped forward to the microphone. Julia glanced casually at him, her deepest attention still with Ellie, whose cheeks were flushed, eyes wide with a certain distracted pleasure Julia had seen on the faces of other performers who had outdone themselves, gone beyond some limit that had always stopped them before. Meanwhile, Anthony was talking about roses. He held two long-stemmed flowers, each wrapped in pearly green tissue. "This is for our teacher," he said, bending over the microphone, which had been shortened to Ellie's height. Stiffly, he held a rose in the direction of the wing from which Cynthia Springwell emerged and took the flower graciously. Then he held the other flower out to Ellie. "For our star," he said. "It's not that easy being a star." She grabbed it a little too quickly. Anthony found his mother's eyes and shrugged.

Crowds of children began rushing off the stage, gathering in the aisles to be greeted by parents. Julia moved toward Anthony, but there were so many children between them that they could not touch. They both looked toward Ellie, standing on the brightly lit, empty stage.

"Come down now, it's over, Elinore," called Cynthia Springwell.

Her mother called her too, and then her father, but Ellie remained frozen to the silver trunk of the microphone.

Anthony wiped makeup off his face with a sweaty hand, streaking his cheeks in pink and black, pulled off his jacket, as all the other children were doing, used costumes flung across seats and mothers' arms. "Mom," he whispered frantically across the shoulders of two boys who stood between them, "Ellie won't come down."

If Ellie had been her child, Julia would have had to restrain herself from rushing up to the stage and carrying her off in her arms, protecting her . . . she didn't know from what—some premature redemption, perhaps; some treacherous descent; an inevitable future failure with the power to destroy everything that had gone before. But she would rock the child in her arms with adoration too—for her grace, for her effort. Julia's heart beat fast, her concern for Ellie stirring the memory of what she, herself, had relinquished, making her wonder if some fragment of magic remained for her, or Daniel, or Anthony, a piece of sparkling glass small enough to be handled safely, as yet undestroyed.

Penetrations

They were hanging a South African poet that night. She thought about it while she dressed and drank her coffee. All over the world protests were arranged, voices shouted in newsprint, telegrams, fruitless pleas, righteous indignation. She sat on the southbound IRT on her way to school, correcting papers, thinking about it in the pauses between one student's essay and another. His face came back to her, the dark, serious face she'd seen in *The New York Times.* Deep crevices lining the cheeks. She couldn't tell from the slightly blurred photo if they were lines of age or ritual.

At Twenty-third Street she returned the essays to their folder and concentrated on the poet. He was ready to die for freedom, he said in a message from his cell. But waiting for the hangman, perhaps he was thinking of his children, or his old mother who had been haunting the prison walls for days, refusing to leave, telling the guards: Kill me if you want to. He's my son. Perhaps he cried. Perhaps he was as scared as she would be in his place. Julia began to cry.

It was not odd in itself, to cry this way about the death of a poet thousands of miles away. Many people would cry if the South African government went through with the hanging. And Julia too had once been a writer. She cried for the poet and for the power of honest language, which could still frighten governments, even in this nuclear age. But in her country, books—like certain elegant plastics—had become so expensive, and a few writers so valuable, that small contracts dwindled and many writers stopped writing, since they had to get jobs, raise children and there wasn't much time left over. Julia was one of those who had stopped.

Now, here was this poet being killed for his words. It would not have been odd for her to cry over such a thing, except that Julia had not cried over anything for several years. She wondered at her tears which flowed in fast streams down her cheeks, causing other passengers to look at her uncomfortably. The woman next to her opened her black canvas bag and handed her a blue perfumed tissue. Julia nodded her appreciation and blew her nose.

The day was unusually hectic, leaving little time to think about anything besides classes, conferences with students, a faculty meeting. But there was one ten-minute period, when she was on line in the cafeteria, an egg-salad sandwich in one hand, a cold diet soda in the other, when the African poet's face came back to her, and right there on line, just as she reached the cashier and held out her five-dollar bill, she nearly cried again.

On the subway going home in the evening, Julia stood near the door, crushed between a tall man and a woman in a fur coat. She forced her eyes downward, focusing on a tiny space of floor in order to avoid leaning her forehead on the man's chest or eating the woman's fur. Usually she was intensely aware of other bodies, other hands touching hers, preferring to risk falling than keep her hand on a crowded pole where some man might cover her fingers and she would have to wonder if it were an accident or a nasty invitation to seduction. Suddenly, though, Julia realized that two hands were sandwiching hers on the pole that she had grasped, unaware. Warily, she looked up from the hands, up the arms, to the faces. One belonged to a young woman whose other arm sheltered two small children, pulling them to her side as the train rocked and bumped along the tracks. The other hand, however, belonged to an older, handsome man whose eyes, when Julia reached them, met her own. He smiled, warmly. Glancing at the rope of hands between them, she realized he could not know her eyes belonged to the hand he pressed so firmly on the pole. She smiled back at him. And this was the second thing that happened that day that Julia knew was odd. For years, she'd felt a drumming anxiety whenever she was in the presence of strange or barely known men, so that she learned to turn her eyes quickly from a man on the street, an acquaintance, especially if she were attracted to him. Once she had been a passionate woman. Often, she would cry during sex from the sheer enormity of the pleasure of connection. But for years she'd made love with her husband only occasionally. She thought of it as sexual amnesia. It wasn't that she didn't want sex. Rather, there was something she couldn't remember about sex, some aspect of desire she'd lost her knowledge of, and this loss made her unable to contemplate sex for months at a time. Yet here she was, smiling at this dark-haired stranger, noticing the pleasing muscles at the base of his neck just beneath the line of the dark blue collar of his shirt.

The train emptied out somewhat at Seventy-second Street, but the man next to her remained, still smiling. So Julia rushed out onto the platform and entered another car farther up the line. Finding a seat, she leaned against the heated plastic, determined to pull herself together so she could discuss the issue of the South African poet with her children at dinner—taking care that they not be spared this most recent lesson in their moral and political education to which she paid such obsessive attention. Just as she was worrying that Anthony might be upset by the execution, a tall bony man walked toward her down the central aisle. He was dressed in thick, layered rags, which, by now, were to all urban dwellers the sign of homelessness. But his rags were thicker than any she had seen, so that while his face and hands indicated frailty, his body, layered many times with filthy sweaters and coats, appeared husky, shapeless, and oddly comforting, like an old down quilt. She looked away from him, as other passengers were doing, but she felt him stop near her seat and look down at her. He did nothing, only remained before her, staring. Finally, she returned his gaze. His age could not easily be determined, but Julia thought he might be young. There were no lines etched into his dark brown skin. His lips were smooth. And his chin line was sharp, reminding her of the sharp angles she so loved in the facial structures of her sons. His hair was characteristically matted, long and tangled into sections that must once have been braids. As soon as she looked up at him, he opened his coat, pulling apart layers of clothing like a thick curtain, baring a thin, beautiful chest covered sparsely with tiny black curls. Quickly, she returned her eyes to her lap and shifted away from him on her seat. He remained, however, despite her discomfort; because of it, perhaps. He stood before her, holding his layers of shirts and sweaters opened, exposing his naked chest, as if it were a work of art containing some hidden message she was expected to see. As soon as the train pulled into her station, she rushed out the door. She breathed deeply, closed her eyes to regain her composure.

So intensely were Julia's thoughts focused on these things—the South African poet, the crying, the handsome man smiling at her, the homeless man with the bared chest—that she crossed the street against the light and was startled into ordinary consciousness by the loud honking of a horn. Why had all these things happened in one day? Or did they happen every day, the only thing that made them special this day being the quality of her noticing? Someone jerked her across the street. "Watch where you're going, honey," he said. Julia leaned against the mailbox and adjusted her coat. She forced herself to pay attention to the street as she headed for the fruit and vegetable stand at the end of the block, where she would buy fresh broccoli and the large blueberry muffins Anthony and Daniel liked so much.

For weeks Anthony had been angry at her, an anger that she knew from her experience with Daniel would be chronic and periodic for years to come. But Daniel and Julia had been angry at each other periodically ever since he was two. Her older son was so much like her, Julia felt, he had to extend his anger between them, a heavy tool inserted in a small crack to break a lock. When his anger escalated during the early years of adolescence, Julia was used to it. It was only a difference in degree. "I get angry at you, but I love you very much," she and Daniel had been assuring each other for as long as she could remember.

But Anthony's love had never been forced by strong ambivalence into the security of flexibility. Until recently, he still curled up next to her each evening, a physical requirement before he could sleep. He stroked her hair, told her she was beautiful. Sometimes he wrote poems which he showed her in secret. But she had encouraged him to take pride in the short emotional explosions he scratched on pads and napkins. She typed them, showing him how they achieved a new meaning when placed carefully on a page. She bought him a white notebook in which to file the poems and wrote his name on the cover. Then suddenly he stopped embracing her. His kisses were perfunctory. He fought with her over the details of housekeeping chores, over the need for a hat in the rain. For weeks she said nothing, knowing she must let him do this, feeling like a lover who knows a passionate affair is about to end and watches with a strange distance that is sacrifice, resignation, and protection all at once. Years ago, Julia would have been ashamed to speak, even to herself, of the passion she felt for her sons, the way in which language, when she spoke of them, reflected the emotions of erotic love. But shame was no longer equal to the task of covering this truth: the children had changed her life. By the very purity of their dependence on her, they had demanded everything she could give, which was often insufficient. Between the two—the giving and the insufficiency—she had been tied to them for years by her deepest attention. And attention—the willingness to look continually, to not turn away, to move around contours, touching, standing back, trying to comprehend the singular meaning of a line, a word, another mind (all were equally mysterious to her, equally compelling)—that *regard,* or attention, was all she knew of any kind of love. "Want to come shopping with me?" she'd asked Anthony, trying to entice him into one of their old favorite activities. They would walk down Broadway together, stopping haphazardly in various stores, holding hands, talking about all the things that cluttered their equally active minds. But he had refused. "I don't mean to hurt your feelings, Mom. But it's kind of boring," he said, and turned away.

She had never actually said to herself: I will not cry again—after all those years during which she had cried so often and intensely she had decided it was remarkable that tears were never used up, but produced in an infinite supply until death, like waste products, or blood. Often, she wished she could cry but succeeded only in making short, high-pitched sounds, like a wounded dog. Hearing the dog sounds, Bruce would think she was crying. He would run his fingers across her cheeks, hoping for tears. But she would be dry-eyed, and they would turn onto their backs, stare at the ceiling, both of them oddly disappointed. She had learned to be satisfied with heat as a biological reaction to pain. Heat rushed through her body while a cold sweat broke out on her face and neck. "Are you upset?" Bruce would ask sometimes, when he knew she was thinking about how she used to write, or after she'd had a fight with one of the boys or with him. And she got used to answering, he to hearing, "No, I'm just hot."

Julia waited as the cashier weighed the broccoli and tomatoes, rang up soy sauce, muffins, white squares of tofu floating like unnaturally geometrical fish entrapped in the cloudy water of the plastic bag.

She *would* watch the news with Anthony and Daniel, she decided as she shifted the groceries to one arm and rang for the elevator. Anthony might be upset, but he had to be hardened, encouraged to become more like his father. She could become furious at Bruce for his capacity to endure disaster—as if he expected nothing from the world but injustice and disappointment. "That's not it at all," he would tell her. "I know there's injustice. But there's happiness too. You're the one who only sees the suffering," he accused. She hoped he would come home early enough to watch the news with them, help her explain things to Anthony. She worried about him, still so raw to every feeling, suffering stomachaches, insomnia, what he called his "bad feelings" at every small experience of pain.

When Daniel was younger he too had refused to watch films that depicted suffering, especially stories about American slavery. He couldn't bear the thought of their misery, he said, couldn't stand the thought of a beating or a lynching. But now, at sixteen, he criticized his brother for oversensitivity. "Just do what I do," Daniel instructed when Anthony wept at the state of the homeless in New York, the killing of Martin Luther King which he studied in school, the kidnapped children whose faces stared out from the sides of milk cartons at the breakfast table. "I just watch it," Daniel said, "and I say to myself—I am

41

here. Sitting in my chair. I'm not that person on the screen. You can watch the most violent movies if you learn to do it right. I can watch the absolutely most violent movies in the world and not get scared. I just keep telling myself—it's not me. It's only actors up there."

"That's movies, Daniel. I'm not talking about the movies."

"The homeless aren't actors, Daniel," Julia chided, instantly regretting her words. What Daniel hated most about her, he said, was her endless moralism.

"I know, Mom," he said, anger already lacing his voice. "But still. It's the principle of the thing."

After she unpacked the groceries and changed her clothes, Julia told the boys about the South African poet and that she wanted them to watch the news with her. Anthony looked nervous. "I don't know if I can take it," he said.

"Try," Julia insisted. "We have to know about these things. They aren't going to show him getting killed on TV, Anthony. We have to pay attention."

"I don't even want to think about it," said Anthony.

"I agree with Mom. It's important to know what's going on in the world," said Daniel, and he plopped onto a large chair close to the TV. Julia, always grateful for her older son's rare support, kissed his forehead as she walked by him to sit near Anthony. "Maybe there'll be a reprieve," she said, taking her son's hand.

But when Dan Rather had finished the top story—about a doctor in the West Indies claiming to have a cure for AIDS—and the South African poet's face appeared on the screen, Bruce walked in and said, "He's dead. They killed him today."

There were shots of the prison near Cape Town, high imposing walls of ancient stone. The poet's mother, a small bent woman cloaked in black, walked quickly past the camera. One of her supporters motioned impatiently with his hand: *Leave her alone.*

"I can't stand it." Anthony bolted from the room.

"Oh, God." Daniel sighed impatiently.

And now Julia found herself defending her younger son. "It is terribly painful, and he's very sensitive, Daniel," she said. She coughed, rubbed her eyes. Bruce looked at her—interested—and took a long sip of his wine.

Anthony had remained in the hallway, anxiously eyeing the television screen during a commercial. "Then why'd you make me watch?" he accused her. "I told you I'd be petrified."

They all turned back to the television screen, Daniel and Julia sitting in the living room, Bruce glancing up intermittently as he fixed his dinner, Anthony from the hallway, peeking out, then jumping back behind the wall. The poet's face, an old black-and-white photograph, covered the screen again, and she could see the lines on his cheeks were the ritual scars received in puberty. Then the photograph was replaced by a film of mourners surrounding the poet's mother, his wife, his children. Bishop Tutu was speaking to a crowd of demonstrators. "They killed a poet today," he said.

"I told you I couldn't stand this," Anthony screamed. "Why'd you make me watch this, Mommy! It's all your fault!" He came back into the living room and sat close to his father who was eating his dinner while sitting on the couch.

"It's not you getting killed. I keep telling you, just remember that and you can take anything," Daniel repeated, grabbing an orange juice carton and taking a long gulp.

"Don't drink from the quart," said Julia, trying to change the subject and ward off a fight.

But Anthony screamed at his brother, "Well, I just can't do it. I'm not like you, okay?"

"You've got to learn. How're you gonna get along in

this world?'' said Daniel, a deep-voiced echo of Julia's words.

"Maybe those feelings of Anthony's are important to hang on to," said Bruce.

"Dad!" Daniel shouted, his shoulders hunched forward slightly, his neck stiff with rage at this betrayal. "What do you do? Cry every time there's some injustice in the world?"

"No," Bruce admitted. "But maybe I wish I did."

Anthony smirked through his tears. Daniel walked angrily into the room where, he'd once confessed to Julia, he often cried as much as Anthony did, but privately.

Late that night Anthony called Julia into his room. He was unable to sleep, so filled was he with the bad feeling. She sat on his bed and listened to him cry.

"I know I've been mean to you," he said. "And I don't know why."

Julia forced herself to explain to Anthony that it was natural, he was growing up, pulling away from her.

"I don't want to pull away from you," he wept. "I don't want to grow up," which alarmed Julia, so she whispered to him about how all children had to grow up and become independent of their parents, but she would always be his mother, he would always be her child. She assured him he wouldn't grow up until he was ready, that it was a slow process, just the beginning. That it was exciting, necessary, full of pleasures he could not yet imagine.

A few weeks before, as they'd lounged around the living room on a Sunday afternoon, Daniel had asked whose hand was bigger now, Anthony's or Julia's. Julia had held up her hand, fingers stretched to measure, but Anthony had hidden his behind his back, saying, "I don't want to know."

"Growing up is a good thing," she had told him then. "You can write a poem about it."

"*You* don't write anymore," Anthony said.

44

Now she held his lanky torso across her lap and fingered his thick curls. Soon he quieted down. "I'm scared," he said.

She caressed his head, his face. "I won't let anything bad happen to you," she told him automatically. But she knew he was thinking about the poet.

"I'll always love you best," he whispered in a small boy's voice.

Julia rocked him, knowing he was falling asleep, but she heard the words resonate like a fading echo. She slid him off her lap and tucked him in. She was about to leave the room, but suddenly she was sitting on the floor, her face buried in his quilt, raw with the loss she knew was inevitable and necessary, the loss from which she felt she might never recover and which she nevertheless had to encourage, even insist upon. She berated herself for self-pity. Was her son in prison? Was he dead? She touched Anthony's fingers, now soft with sleep. Still, she kept hearing the echo—I'll always love you best. If it were true, she was frightened; if false, bereft.

She went over to Daniel's bed, where he breathed the rhythmical breaths of the deepest level of sleep, and she sat beside this son whose leaving had been taking place since the day he learned to walk. She felt proud of Daniel's fierce boundaries, for his determination to be different from her. She felt grateful that Daniel had never made her cry with his pubescent rages because he had made it clear for so long that his passion was not her, but the world.

That night, in her deep sleep, Julia felt her life threatened. She tried to awaken, part of her knowing she was dreaming and in the dream was in danger of being killed, part of her still in the dream, succumbing to the imminent attack. She felt Bruce shake her and heard him call her name.

"You're dreaming, honey. You're dreaming."

Finally she pulled herself out of the dream, into the

dark, cool room she had shared with Bruce for twenty years. The beige cotton curtains ballooned with air, then pasted again to the glass. The soothing greens, browns and whites of the room looked deep gray in the semidark. She covered her face with her hands. "I was being killed," she said. As soon as she said it, she remembered—she was not being killed. Someone was taking Daniel from her. It was Daniel who was in danger. He was being dragged or pushed or sucked away, and from the look on his face he had no idea of the danger he was in. Julia had screamed in her dream as Daniel had disappeared.

"In two years he'll be going to college," she whispered to Bruce.

"Who? Daniel? I know. Was that your dream?" His voice cracked slightly with emotion reflecting hers. She turned her back to him but lay very close so that her shoulders and buttocks touched his chest and thighs. He held her and began to lift his hands to her breasts, but she moved away from him.

"I'm sorry," he said.

Then the amnesia broke. She had forgotten the *desire* to be open. Once it had not been a fear, but a yearning.

She almost turned around in the comforting dark of the familiar room, the bed in which her children had been conceived, where she and Bruce had made love hundreds of times, felt themselves to be almost one person, and then more different from each other than from anyone else in the world. She felt lost to him in the cloudy dark, unseen; unseen. She could begin a story with this feeling, she thought—with the African poet, the crying, the bare chest of the homeless man. Like the world pulled Daniel something outside herself was pulling her. But she only raised Bruce's fingers to her lips.

"No, I'm the one who's sorry," she said. "I'm too upset, that's all."

Long ago she would have sunk into sex as a comfort, wanting the moment when she would feel unprotected, completely light, and free. Weeks, even a few days before, she would have felt only heat—that strange, enveloping fever she'd grown used to as a sign that she might be in pain. Now she felt cold, shaken with chills as if she were the young man with the bare chest. She had looked away, but now she rose from her subway seat and held him. He laid his head on her shoulder, and she felt the stressed and tightened muscles in his back. He leaned heavily against her, but she could not remain aloof, and she touched his hair, ran her finger down the swollen vein in his temple, his angular jaw which reminded her of Daniel, of Anthony.

Another Woman

Lying down in the dark next to Bruce, Julia tried to get the feeling she'd once loved of safety, as if all her anxieties were fenced outside a small piece of cultivated land that for one moment seemed to be the entire world. She would have felt, in that moment, a cellular hunger, as for sex, or food, and soon a suspended weightlessness with his flesh touching hers. Instead, she felt heavy and sad and his thigh felt like just another thigh tired from walking and standing and an early morning run. He wouldn't touch her, she knew. Repeated rejections had broken his confidence, veiled his desire. The veil floated between them, then became a heavy curtain—brocade, lined in thick cotton, dark blue. She might have pushed it aside, but that would require raising her hand, parting the folds, using her leaden fingers, hard and frozen. She used to find it easy to speak the truth. Now, she curled behind any barrier; contained, unreachable. Julia imagined the barrier and lowered her head like a bull, ready to plunge. But she didn't remember how. All those lectures she had given people who wanted and feared connection she could give herself now. She was like them now, seeing clearly the advantage of openness; hopelessly closed. She turned over and shadowed Bruce's curved torso. He took her hands and kissed her fingers, then turned toward her again. "Did you write today?" he said, pulling the front of her hair back with his hand.

Julia raised her knees to her chest and bent her face to them. She hadn't written in a year, and still—every month or so—he would ask, Did you write today? As if the months were days, as though she might just start again, without warning. She remained silent, her legs still pulled up to her chest, his arms around her; he kissed her knees. When she didn't respond, he turned onto his back so that she was left alone in her curled-up position, feeling stiff. She straightened out too and massaged her left palm, which ached, with her right. She stroked each of her fingers, felt the smoothness of the short nail, turned her silver ring around, held her own hand again. She wanted to let go and reach for him. She imagined the feel of his thighs, the soft hair between his legs that spread sparsely over his belly like tufts of sea grass leading back from a dune. She felt the bulk of his smooth chest come over her, him entering her while he covered her forehead and eyes with his palm. She heard his high-pitched moan and remembered when her hunger rolled inside her, out of her mouth, breaking contours with its dangerous fluidity. She realized she was grasping her own hand. The fingers were numb.

Bruce turned onto his stomach now, always his last position before he fell asleep. He patted her shoulder, fingered the strap of her nightgown. The nightgown had been a present from her best friend. It had arrived in the mail for no particular occasion. "You need this," the card said. It was made of soft cotton, the straps delicate bands of thread, across the front a border of green-and-blue embroidery. It was nearly transparent, and although Julia loved to sleep in it, she hated the sight of herself in the hall mirror—the way the aging lines of her body were visible through the white.

"I feel frightened," she whispered, thinking Bruce was asleep.

"You do?" he said.

As he turned to face her she turned back the other way so that he enclosed her torso, and that was how they fell asleep.

Julia felt so changed she could no longer predict her reactions to ordinary things. She cried when she bumped her head slightly on an overhead shelf. When she thought her feelings would have been hurt, she turned blithely around to stir the spinach. When she looked into the mirror she was surprised, each morning again, to discover her hair was almost completely gray. She was only forty-three, but in the mirror she saw her grandmother's face.

Finally, after months of scanning the drugstore shelves of hair dye, she dared to ask the saleswoman about the various colors and kinds. "You see, I don't want anything permanent," she said, shivering at the thought of a six-month-long choice of auburn or velvet black. "Just so I can see. . . ."

The saleswoman regarded Julia's hair carefully. "You would want a brown tone, right?" She plucked a silver bottle from the shelf. "This," she said, handing it to Julia.

Julia touched the ends of her hair, fingering curls, when she said, "Brown, yes, my hair is brown."

"Was." The saleswoman smiled, a doctor giving bad news in a palliative of diagnostic accuracy. "Take this. You'll love the change. A lovely ash brown." She caressed her own opaque black waves. "Rejuvenated. That's how you'll feel."

"But I want to be able to get it out if I don't like it. You know, if I make a mistake?"

"You can wash it out. Guarantee." She pointed to the fine print.

Julia paid for the dye and shoved it into her purse, looking around like a girl shoplifting bobby pins. "You're sure I can wash it out?" she turned to say.

"Like watercolors," the saleswoman said. "I promise."

When she got home, Julia stripped off her clothing immediately, nervously, so that she caught her hair in the zipper of her blouse and had to cut off several strands that had become hopelessly tangled in the tiny silver teeth. She went into the bathroom and began to paint. Ten minutes later she was ash brown again, every damp, curly strand. People told her she had a young face, but now it seemed that way to her. She jumped into the shower and washed it out. In the mirror was the confirmation of the saleswoman's promise: she was herself again. So once more she began to paint. She squeezed the mixture into her hands, rubbed it into her scalp. Gray turned brown again, down the sides, under layers, wispy bangs. The spray bottle was hard to direct into her palm, however, a great spurt of liquid came out at once, and when she was done she saw, dismayed, that dye stains were all over the bathroom. Brown rivulets ran into streams down the white tile. Large splotches of brown, hasty Rorschachs for an interpretive psychiatric eye, decorated the sink. A streak of brown lightning tore across the ceiling. Julia grabbed the washcloth and rubbed the Rorschachs and rivers off the porcelain tiles and pink walls. But she didn't pay close attention, so enthralled was she with her ash brown curls, so tiny tributaries and edges of butterflies and the entire lightning streak remained, evidence of her transformation, her witch's brew. Wait until they come home, she thought. Wait 'til they see.

When she heard the first knock at the door, she was right there to open it. She turned on the hall light, saying nothing, standing in Anthony's way.

"Yo," he said, and kissed her cheek. Then he walked around her into his room. Julia followed him, watched him throw down his enormous bag of books, stood before him as he pulled off his weighty high-tops. "Is there anything to eat?" he asked. "I'm starving."

"Chocolate milk," she mumbled, smile fading, "and that Vermont cheddar you like."

Anthony left the room and headed for the kitchen.

While she was fixing dinner, she heard Bruce's key in the door. "Hi," she nearly shouted when he came in.

"Hi," he answered, looking into pots on the stove. "You look nice. Have a good day?"

She followed him into their room, as she had followed Anthony, and sat down on their bed as he hung up his jacket, changed into sweat pants and a T-shirt, dumped his change into a blue clay bowl Daniel had made in the fifth grade.

"Anything important happen?" she asked, looking down at the *Times,* brown locks facing him.

"Another city official indicted." He started to smile. "What's wrong with you? Did something happen?"

"Why?" she asked innocently. "Why do you ask? Does something seem changed?"

"No." He raised his eyebrows, confused by the conversation, and turned on the news.

A wave of resentment passed through her, warning her with the familiar satisfaction it left in its wake. Once she would have pointed angrily to her hair, accused him of indifference. Now, she kept her feelings to herself. Besides, he looked confused, not indifferent. And how odd it must seem for him, she forced herself to imagine, to be shut out of her feelings after so many years of having the power (no matter that it was a power of which he was unaware) to take an interest in some of her revelations, ignore others. More than odd, she thought, noticing the slight slope of his shoulders, the way his eyebrows knit together questioningly when he looked at her. She tapped him on the shoulder from behind. "Are you feeling lonely?" she asked.

"In a way," he said. "Is Daniel home yet?"

When Daniel arrived, she thought, he would notice instantly, and then everyone would talk about it. But they were already eating when he walked in, late and exhausted from football practice. He sat down, barely looking at anyone. After shoving several spoonfuls of chicken and rice into his mouth, he looked at Julia and said, "I'm starving." Then he began to tell them about a paper he had to do that night on D. H. Lawrence's *Sons and Lovers*. "My idea is this," he said, placing open palms on the table before him. "Everyone always thinks the father in the story is so stupid, you know, such a bad guy. He's supposed to be brutal, and I realize he is totally insensitive. . . ."

"Dad! I want that piece!" Anthony yelled as Bruce retrieved an especially crisp piece of chicken.

"Well, don't spear me with the fork," Bruce said, settling for a large helping of rice.

"Can I have the juice? And do you want me to get it myself or will you?" Anthony asked.

Julia had forbidden Anthony, who had trouble sitting still for more than five minutes at a time, from getting up for any reason during dinner, so now she was forced to serve him. She brought the quart of juice to the table.

"Does anyone mind if I finish? I mean, is anyone interested in what I'm saying here?" Daniel said loudly, angry eyes directed at Anthony.

"It's not my fault. I just wanted juice. And Dad took all the chicken."

"I did not take *all* the chicken. Just the piece you wanted."

"Can Daniel finish?" Julia asked angrily. It was an ordinary disruption, but something about the way Daniel was not being heard bothered her with special intensity. She felt anxious, as if she were about to shout. But she had sworn not to shout anymore. "So what do you think?" she said to him in a tight, controlled tone. "About the father in *Sons and Lovers?*"

"Well, I think of course the father is brutal, but it's really the mother's fault. I mean, his insensitivity, his brutality—all of it's a reaction, really, to her snobbery. She never loved him. And she always tries to put him down to his son."

"There's plenty to call her fault in the book, Daniel, without blaming her for his problems, too," Julia began, but, as she might have known, her disagreement provoked Daniel's anxiety, which threatened to come out as anger.

"No," he said with a shake of his head. "You have to be honest about this, Mom. It's her fault. The son and the father would have been close if not for her. No. Don't say I'm wrong. That's my thesis."

Julia glanced quickly at Anthony, whose eyes met hers. But then he looked down at his rice. She pressed her lips together, folded her hands in her lap. She leaned back in her chair. All these were gestures she had constructed to contain her words when unnamed emotions threatened explosions. *Did Daniel feel that way, then? That she stood between him and Bruce? Was he angry at her so often because he was too much like her? Or was she angry at him because he was too much like Bruce, intimidating her with his confidence, mercilessly self-contained?* "Interesting, Daniel. An interesting idea," she told him as he picked up the orange juice carton to take a long swig. "Would you please not drink from the quart?" she said too loudly, and pushed a glass toward him roughly.

"Chill out, Mom. I'm finishing the juice anyway." He crushed the carton with his hand to prove his point. "Oh! I just thought of a great line. He has to get away from his mother—in *Sons and Lovers,* I mean—before she eats him alive. It's kind of cliché, I admit, but it's right to the point. Will you type my paper when I'm done with it tonight, Mom?"

She forced herself to nod and rose to help Anthony clear the table, then could not restrain herself from one last, direct effort. "Notice anything different?" she asked, running her fingers through her hair.

They all looked around. "You changed the living room around again!" Daniel announced, amazed, as he viewed the old furniture, unchanged except for a new day's layer of dust.

All that night, she tossed and turned in her bed until a nightmare (images of snow, a heavy blizzard) woke her to a cacophony of critical voices. Daniel's of her—why couldn't she be a calmer person? he wanted to know. One of her students who was "sick unto death"—she said—of "revision, revision, revision." Bruce's pained look when she began to describe her anxieties about the children or worried too much when they were late coming in at night. Voices of old enemies, lost friends, an ambitious critic who'd once accused her of overintensity, self-involvement, and a too autobiographical voice. All these voices came into her head in the middle of the night until she heard the original voices, cackling sounds in her ears, indecipherable language, companions of her childhood solitude in which she was never fully, happily alone. To quiet the voices, she got out of bed, turned on a small blue lamp in the living room, and paced the floor as she remembered her father doing when she was a child. Back and forth she went, a specter, she thought bitterly, muttering to herself, as she recalled him doing, her long white nightgown reflecting the shadows of the night.

"Why do you pace?" she had asked him repeatedly when she was a child, awakened by his nighttime trekking, then a teenager, annoyed. "I'm trying to adjust," was all he said. To being a widower, she imagined first; then, to getting old. But what was she trying to become, with her sleek brown hair? She sat down again, pulled a long strand in front of her eyes marveling at the color, and remembered her grandmother again.

She is talking as always, words shouted, muttered to

others, to herself—curses and complaints, a lifelong, futile attempt to make her children and grandchildren understand her life. "The womb is crying at its emptiness," was her analysis of Julia's first menstrual cramps, this addendum after the lights were out and more modern explanations had been made. After Julia's mother died, she moved in with another daughter and son-in-law with whom she battled for years in dinner table skirmishes. "He never talks to me direct," she would complain every Tuesday night when she came to sleep over so Julia's father could go out. "He never looks at me and calls me by my name. He says, Doris, tell your mother to pass the meat. Doris, your mother needs bread. At most, he looks at me and without any kind of addressing of a person he says, So how's your cold? I don't answer. In fifteen years he doesn't use my name. Let him call me Mother, I tell Doris. Let him call me Annie. Let him call me son of a bitch, but let him call me something."

Grandma Annie looked tranquil in her coffin, like a younger version of herself. Julia ran her tongue over her lips, salty wet from tears, recalling the hot water she used to lick off the big nipples when they played Mama and Baby in the bath. But her offerings of a long drained breast were occasional. Mostly, she wept. Her legs ached from arthritis. Her fingers swelled with the rains. Her gums bled profusely whenever she brushed her teeth or ate an apple. Her heart ached for her dead children. A half century after she'd left her rabbi father's home, she still vomited at even the distant smell of bacon. *Oy, gevalt,* she'd moan over and over on her baby-sitting night as Julia pretended to be asleep. "And where is your father tonight?" she'd intone, undeceived. "Out with women, and your mother only two years dead. Try to find out, *ketzeleh.* God forbid he finds another wife. What will happen to you then, or to me?" Images would accost her, images she never hesitated to impart to her granddaughter—the two of them wandering unclaimed through the streets of this enormous western shtetl, taken in, perhaps, by nuns, no one else available, struggling fruitlessly to preserve dignity among the goyim, or at the very least left to the questionable mercies of Doris and her husband. "And don't tell your father I talk to you like this," she'd warn, echoing the injunction of keeping the ups and downs of menstruation to oneself: "Openness is one thing, but at this a man will faint in disgust." She'd cry, and her sobs eventually assumed the rhythm of a song. *Tium nai a notch* (dark is the night)—*Ya vdalekia ot Doma* (and I am far from home). And another song for which Julia once made the mistake of requesting a translation: *You ask me, my friend, how old am I. I tell you I do not know. If living means trouble, then I've lived so long, I've lived for many a year. But if living means sharing the slightest bit of joy, then I wasn't yet born.* "So you wanted to know? That's what it means," she finished as Julia hunched beneath the blue-and-white-flowered quilt, watching her grandmother's prone body on the other bed. Her arm, strangely youthful from the elbow down, stretched back over her shoulder. Her thick white hair, loosened from its habitual pins, feathered over the pale blue pillow.

Julia winced at the memories of her grandmother's needs and claims, her father's misery, never unexpressed. Ghetto habits—sorrows so unmalleable, only sound provided relief. *What is it, medeleh, tell me, tell me, tell me,* was what she heard throughout her childhood in response to her slightest frown. Julia heard herself humming the old Yiddish songs, and, frightened of falling into some sort of pit between the pacing and the humming, she returned to bed.

The following morning, having assured herself the first shower by rising at six and returning her hair to its usual gray (some strands retained their darker color, she noticed happily), she began reading her students' work with a familiar sense of relief. By the time two hours had passed and Bruce and the boys were beginning to depart for the day, she was thoroughly immersed in the exciting risks Leila was taking after so many stories that followed a successful but by now schematic plan. "Switch to the first person—just try it as an exercise," she'd advised when Leila came to her office the week before complaining of block. Now, here was this beautiful first-person narrative by Leila's fictional self, a voice that pursued meaning yet did not shrink from doubt. "But it won't fit in with the voice of my stories," Leila had warned. Her dark eyes focused on Julia's, inviting her best thinking, and this is what she loved about teaching, what made it easier and yet somehow more satisfying than the writing she once did herself—the constant need to encourage, collaborate with another mind. "Try it anyway," Julia had advised, with only a touch of guilt that she counseled so confidently what she would no longer do herself. But she did feel confident with her students, never heard her own voice as if from another mouth as she did when she spoke of her own writing and, lately, when she spoke to her sons.

She wrote a lengthy response to Leila's story, commending the new, more exposed voice as the right track, notwithstanding the slightly problematic structure. "You have those skills," Julia wrote. "You can retrieve them on a later draft."

Just as she was beginning to edit Mathew's work, Bruce came in to say good-bye. She kissed him warmly, the intensity of their morning embrace, she noticed lately, in proportion to the depth of the breach between them at night. As if each were another person—some smarter and freer twin—apologizing for incapacity, the distances of marriage, the disappointments of middle age. "Have a good day, sugar," he said, using the old, now rare endearment of their better years.

Mathew was writing about a painful conflict with his father, a story he'd begun the previous semester from the

point of view of the family maid, an immigrant from Ec-
uador, a forty-year-old mother of five. He'd become
blocked after the fifth page and remained there for ten
weeks. At the very end of the term, Julia had finally insisted: Do it from the son's point of view. (She did not
say, Do it from *your* point of view, trying to keep up the
fictions of fiction.) Still—"It'll be too autobiographical,"
Mathew had complained. "I'll be so involved with the
voice, I'll lose track of the form and style." But desperation had made him agree and now, his voice personal and
resonant, he was finishing the novel at a clip. Leila and
Mathew were two of her favorite students. Working on
their fiction was medicinal. She was old enough to be
their mother. But she was not their mother.

She dressed calmly (black skirt, black sweater) to hide,
or express, the remnants of the night. She tucked the sides
of her gray hair back with tortoiseshell combs—a youthful
look—and applied dark rose blush to her winter-sallowed
cheeks. All the way downtown on the subway, her eyes
hidden by the darkest of sunglasses—which she'd begun
wearing to blur her view of the increasing number of rats
on the tracks—she thought with pleasure about Leila's
new voice, Mathew's proliferation of pages, until sorrows
of many sorts retreated to the back of her mind: Bruce's
loneliness; Daniel's increasing annoyance at her the closer
he came to his last year of living at home; Anthony, who
even a year before would never have failed to notice a
change in the color of her hair; the beggar woman on her
corner who each morning and evening stretched out an
emaciated hand.

The first student who came in for office hours was
Vicky, looking distraught. "I know I give the impression
of being in control of everything, but I'm telling you
Julia . . ." She shook her head as if talking about a younger
sibling. "I'm like totally falling apart." She pulled her
knees up to her chin as she settled into the raggedy, com-

fortable easy chair. Her long, flowered print skirt fell in graceful folds around her ankle-high leather boots. When Julia first met her, Vicky's hair had been half-fuchsia, half coal black. The next semester it was a yellowish white. (Julia remembered the yellow white of her grandmother's hair and, fleetingly, the sound of her warnings and complaints.) She blinked and returned her attention to Vicky, whose hair was a natural brown again. Julia ran her hand through her hair, pushed against the back of the chair, as if trying to escape. Perhaps if this had been someone other than Vicky, she thought, she would be sympathetic but cool, send the student off to the director of student life with a Recommendation for Counseling form. (So many of them needed counseling. There were broken love affairs, suicide attempts, abortions, a first homosexual affair. There was drinking, and drugs, and for the girls eating disorders of every description. They crowded the faculty offices in this small, intimate college, seeking, Julia felt at times, nothing so much as adult conviction. They sat themselves down with their stories and stared at you, waiting for some sense to be made.) But Julia's discomfort with her secondary role as counselor never seemed to move beyond the abstract to the actual encounter. She could not resist Vicky's need.

The wall behind Vicky was cluttered with memos, calendars of events, all surrounding a large flower painting suggesting space and sun. A line of postcard photographs of women writers stretched across another wall. On a small square of space between two bookshelves was a colored print of Donatello's *Mary Magdalene,* looking gaunt and resigned. The shelves were filled with books by women writers, books about women and fiction. At the end of the day, Julia liked to stand by the window and stare at these shelves, scanning the titles, the disorganized, incomplete array of the history of women writing over almost two hundred years. Of course, the incompleteness was not entirely accidental. Julia preferred memoirs, confessional poetry, classic novels in which contemporary critics had revealed passionate subtexts about female power, madness, and loss. She had some of the critical works too, so she could pluck the right book off the shelf to lend to even the most mildly interested student.

"I'm not always the in-control person I seem to be," Vicky was saying. She touched her eyes with her finger as if she were fighting off tears, but on the contrary, Julia thought—she was checking for tears hopefully, trapped behind her habitual strengths. "I'm afraid I'm an alcoholic," she declared in a detached, clinical voice. "I drink every day. I'm not doing my work. And I don't eat. The anorexia's back. I'm thinking of signing myself into a hospital, Julia, taking a leave from school."

They talked for an hour. Julia asked questions, offered sympathy as she might to a contemporary, a friend. She tried to find out if Vicky's parents would help—("No, they think I'm exaggerating, just complaining as usual"); if Vicky had gotten professional help—(Julia was no therapist, she wanted that clear). She tried to provide a little distance by reminding Vicky of how common, even ancient, her troubles were. "You don't have to be in control of everything, always the good girl," she told her. Vicky smiled but stared down at the gray carpet and fiddled with the laces of her boots. The desire to prove virtue through a faultless self-control, and the underside—the impulse to be insane so the hungry voices could shout—was as formidable now, Julia saw again and again, as it was for the women they read about in class, Victorian governesses and mad, isolated wives. "How do you feel after you eat?" she asked, worried about nutrition.

"Like the most disgusting thing in the world," answered Vicky. "Like I am totally out of control."

Much later in the afternoon, Julia was seated in her department chairman's office having trouble concentrating on a meeting. She was thinking about Vicky's doctor appointment, wondering if she would take a leave from school. Then her thoughts turned to the freshmen she had just taught. With the younger students, confessions and feelings were only too evident and out in the open. She had only to define the first assignments as autobiography and their life stories came rolling out onto the page. What they never seemed to have considered before (it was remarkable to her) was that personal writing needed order and restraint too, that clarity and truth were values that applied—or failed to apply—to knowledge of the self as well as to knowledge of the world. With these students, she was always pushing structure until, inevitably, some of them would accuse her of being too rigid (self-confident, they sometimes called it, trying to be nice)— not appreciative enough of the role of inspiration or passion in art. She could figure no way out of the dilemma. Every time she tried to eliminate or soften her insistence on craft with eighteen-year-olds, they abandoned nearly every rule of coherence and focus. "Give 'em an inch . . ." she may have muttered, because Steve, the chairman of the literature and writing program, looked at her intensely and said, "Julia? Are you here?"

She nodded, avoiding his eyes which always disturbed her slightly, the intensity of his stare stirring up memories of passions of various kinds. She had wanted to write about everything she learned. Once, there had been no fear of exposure or hint of shame. She thought of Steve's body, of old and shameful hungers. Then she thought of heavy curtains, and she breathed calmly again.

When she began to pay attention, she realized they were all talking about the problem that worried her. The younger writing students needed discipline, yet one did not want to force them into some old-fashioned straight-jacket of grammatical rule and structural shape until their imaginations were sacrificed to form, just so they could handle its demands. (Anthony had begun to get A's on his English papers, he'd told her the other night, when he figured out that if he didn't try to say anything too inter-esting or complicated, he could organize the paper ex-actly the way his teacher wanted him to.) Her colleagues debated the issue, and she listened with interest for some time. But then she found herself retreating again to the back of her mind, to Vicky, to the sound of Leila's con-fessional voice, to herself trying to change and at the same time changing without any conscious control—from one sort of woman to another. She felt surrounded by silence, a disturbing yet sensuous feeling of the world going dim.

She looked up to find Steve staring at her again. She straightened on her chair and contributed to the conver-sation. But his eyes lingered in that maddening, confusing way, which was when she remembered her dream from the night before.

She was lost in a strange neighborhood in the middle of one of those occasional New York snowstorms that transforms the city into a remote and eerie place. No one was on the street. She was frightened of being lost in the blizzard, peering around her for outline, a familiar land-mark, the apartment of an old friend. But there was no shape, no suggestion of solidity to ground her. And then, in the blinding, paradoxical blizzard—a darkness made of white—she is suddenly aware of silence. Cars are slowed to a creeping pace, then the entire avenue is empty except for one pedestrian, slow-moving and hunched into a sil-houette, crossing the street. The silence is audible, and so seductive she feels she might slip through it (as though silence were a place) and not be found again. It was in that moment of stillness, when she opened to the silence with as little will as a woman about to be caressed in a long desired and interminably postponed embrace, that the nightmare heartbeat broke through the dream and woke her to the critical voices, the resurrected memory of Grandma Annie.

When the meeting broke up, Julia spoke privately to Vicky's adviser, repeating the chilling words about being disgusting and out of control. As she quoted her language, she felt Vicky's feeling, and a wave of self-loathing passed through her so forcefully that she had to sit down to manage the nausea. For a moment she heard the recriminating voices, right there in the office. But quickly she thought of her students, how she reminded them that critical voices could be one's own better judgment warning of excess, the need for perspective. She told every writing class about George Eliot developing a dialogue with those voices until she could rely on their warnings as well as banish them when they'd taken a wrong turn. "The self that self restrains," Eliot had called it. Julia had typed the phrase and taped it above her desk. Now, she thought happily of how Mathew and Leila were able to suspend their formal skills, or lower them, rather, a safety net under increasingly confident acrobats. She detained her departing colleagues to tell them this story, to describe Mathew's and Leila's recent work. The others listened, nodded their heads, the future of the disgruntled freshmen optimistically predicted in the achievements of those other two.

Later, emerging from the close, urine-smelling air of the subway into the early November night, she removed her dark glasses while she handed the homeless woman her daily dollar and forced herself to look into her eyes. But having forfeited for a moment the slight film of distance she could affect so easily with the world, she looked quickly away. Something in those eyes sucked her down, beneath pity and choice. She felt as she did when she read Anthony's recent poems about famine in Africa, Ethiopian children's bodies and spirits mangled by starvation. She would respond with her own memories of hunger of another sort, and then worry—was she using them? the suffering multitudes in comparison to whom her starvation was nothing, the gluttony of the habitually filled? But she could not deny the sense of kinship she felt;—along with guilt for her presumption—the shame, as if it were herself so hungry, arm outstretched, nearly prone on the filthy street.

No, she thought, I will act toward Daniel and Anthony as I do toward my students, respectful of their boundaries, wary of the excesses of maternal love. And I will be restrained with Bruce, silent in the face of his difference from me. She said all this to herself half-aloud while getting the mail, mentally planning the most filling dinner for the boys.

It was early enough for her to have a bath before they all came home, and she brought a candle into the bathroom, ran hot water, turned off the light. Gray dusk, colored darkly by the city night, created patterns on the pale pink walls. The room was small, bitterly efficient, as was every space in these new high-risers, no architectural flourish—an arch, a molding—to give a context of physical complexity to human life. One had to build all that in. She had painted stripes of color near the ceiling, suggesting a molding. She had covered one entire wall with mirrors of different sizes, beautifully framed. She noticed the brown lightning streak still on the ceiling, and standing on the rim of the bathtub, feeling annoyed, she washed it away. She immersed herself in the steaming water, placed her open palms on her breasts, the wet washcloth across her raised knees. Every molecule of air between herself and the world felt as brittle as if she could feel what Anthony had informed her was the physical truth he had learned in his biology class: that no one really touches anything or anyone. There is always a molecular wall, however infinitesimally slight, between the hand and the object it seems to be touching.

Julia imagined painting an old-fashioned narrow window in the dull, tiny bathroom. The window would contain eighteen small panes, each bordered by a wrought-iron frame. The frame would be half-opened, and pushing in all around it would be dark green leaves—maple and oak—a plethora of undisciplined leaves, crowding in richly all spring and summer (she ran her hands slowly over her body from neck to knee), turning stunning colors in the fall, and in the winter their branches would bare themselves for her, a threaded line drawing outlined in crystalline ice. She submerged her head, and the water washed out what was left of the dye, turning her hair as white as her grandmother's. As her ears filled with water she heard the old song.

Fictions of Home

*This is a world in which the first thing one sees is
a woman writing.*
> —*Ursula K. Le Guin,*
> "A Woman Writing, or The
> Fisherwoman's Daughter"

*A woman sat at her dining room table and stared across
an empty notebook page, a pen held tightly in her fingers. Perhaps she would draw as she used to when she
was a child, instead of write these words which turned
dead as soon as the letters were framed. Worse than dead.
They looked like meaningless patterns of sticks, or at best
letters and language belonging to a list more than a story:
referential, thin, insignificant.*

A woman with a pen in her hand and a notebook before
her sits at a table of unstained oak whose simplicity gives
her a feeling of peace. She stares out a window at another
window in which, every so often, another woman—first
in a slip, then a blouse and skirt, then a coat—makes coffee, drinks it, places the cup in the sink. The pen remains
still, although the woman in the apartment across the way,
especially when she was in her slip, has the large breasts
and wide hips that for a moment cause Julia to want to
describe her. She moves around her kitchen with the air
of unconsciousness one uses at home. She reaches for a
cup without thinking: the cups are on the left shelf. The
hand knows where the cup is. And while she pours hot
coffee into a red mug, she absently turns on the hot water.

She needn't look to see which tap is hot, which cold. Julia watches, a voyeur noticing details of a woman at home. But what if she goes on with the story? Julia wonders, tapping the table with her pen and closing her notebook. The moment she moves beyond description there will be trouble. She knows this from trouble in the past. All sorts of complexities will arise, causing headaches and confusion. Her own life will shadow the other woman's, making her notice things about herself she can do without. Another story may gradually intrude until it takes over the one she had meant to tell. Or the story might end up someplace she hadn't planned, forcing into language an insight better left to the comfortable ambiguities of semi-consciousness. There was something about the woman's way of moving, for instance, that suggested efficiency and assertion to which Julia is already negatively comparing herself.

Her apartment is quiet and neat. The walls are a pleasing cream color, not exactly white. Around the room, in rugs and chairs and curtains, are the green and brown tones Julia loves. She looks at the colors, runs open palms across the unstained oak of the table, and watches the woman across the way as she buttons her coat while looking out her kitchen window, perhaps at Julia, then disappears.

She returns her notebook to the shelf above her desk and begins to dress for school. Outside, behind moving layers of various grays in a darkening sky, snow seems to gather and threaten. If there is a storm tonight, Julia thinks, she will be even more resistant than she already is to going to the homeless shelter with Anthony. And all through the day, while she teaches classes and counsels students on their writing projects, she ponders and regrets her commitment to Anthony. Then instantly she feels guilty. Of course she will go with him. Anthony is cornered lately by his contradictory impulses toward suffering. He is obsessed by it, wallpapers his room with posters against every injustice. He writes dozens of poems about starving

African children, all in the first person. Yet he keeps his distance from action of any kind. "It upsets me," he tells her. "I can't sleep at night." So she had called a friend, an activist for the homeless, who suggested a small, carefully screened program in a synagogue in Gramercy Park—not too overwhelming—a good place to begin.

Both Bruce and Daniel will be gone overnight. She will have some time to relax, she thinks as she enters her apartment at the end of the day, before Anthony comes home. She retrieves her journal from the shelf and writes underneath the short description of herself preparing to describe the woman in the window across the way: *I am going to serve dinner to homeless people in a small shelter tonight. With Anthony.*

It is a cold night in the middle of the winter of 1987. Sleet is falling in a thick film, and the streets are deserted. Anthony and Julia walk down Twenty-second Street between First and Second avenues and turn onto the tree-lined block called Gramercy Park East. Number 120, an old synagogue housing a small shelter for the homeless, faces a gated park that can be opened only with keys provided to tenants of the exclusive apartments on the square. It looks to her like a scene from a novel set in old London—moments before the start of a fancy ball or of a grisly murder. Instead, having found themselves to be the first volunteers to arrive, Julia and Anthony wait for a group of homeless people who have been carefully chosen by city shelter managers as being relatively sane and certainly not violent. They are aristocrats of the homeless and allowed to come to this pleasant, large room night after night so that for a few weeks at a time the shelter offers one quality of ordinary homes: there every night, or at least for the allotted ten; predictable, stable.

The volunteers have been welcomed and given instructions by a distinguished-looking black man, the custodian of the synagogue, to whom Anthony virtually bows when he says hello. Then they begin pulling out the cots and arranging them in four rows, placing one cotton sheet at the foot of each, one folded green army blanket, one striped pillow, one cotton pillowcase. Next, they are led into the kitchen to prepare plates of cookies and dough-nuts and to count out paper cups for coffee and tea. Soon, a bus pulls up at the door, and about twenty people, all carrying shopping bags packed with belongings, begin fil-ing in like weary world travelers arrived at last at their hotel having been crowded on the tour bus all afternoon. Julia reaches for Anthony's hand. From the beginning, when they were infants in her arms, or strapped in col-orful corduroy carrying packs to her chest, or leading her (so it seemed at times) down the street in their carriages behind which she obediently pushed, she felt, in addition to whatever resentment of her chores, obligations, the endless attentions they demanded, a sense of safety too whenever she was with them. She was no longer horribly visible—alone in the world—and no longer frighteningly invisible. She was Daniel's, then Anthony's, mother.

There are ten or twelve volunteers this night, more than enough hands to serve the coffee, bring out the few plates of sweets. When the small troop of homeless people walks into the room, the workers stand idly, arms laced uncom-fortably across chests, ridiculous smiling hosts. Within moments, however, the roles are reversed and the work-ers are the guests, useless, even intrusive, as the others walk to their cots and begin fitting sheets over thin mat-tresses, spreading blankets, placing belongings on the floor below. "This isn't a spectator sport, you know," an old man shouts across the room as he tucks in perfect hospital corners.

Anthony turns swiftly on his heels and heads for the kitchen returning a few minutes later armed with napkins and enough paper cups for a battalion. He begins laying out napkins, folded carefully as he has been taught to do but never does at home, each one placed precisely equidistant from the next. Julia watches him and feels a surge of tenderness. She has brought him here to avoid the trauma of a first experience in a huge armory, teeming with sick and desperate people, too much work for the volunteers to manage, hopelessness flattening any possible belief in his power and therefore his responsibility to affect the world. Now, here they are at the other extreme, feeling superfluous. She follows him, straightening the perfectly straight napkins he is arranging on the table. "Will you leave them alone, please? They're fine," he says.

"They'll be sitting down soon," a more experienced volunteer tells them. "You serve them from the table, then sit down and talk."

"Why do we have to serve them?" asks Anthony. "It's not that I mind. I'm just curious."

Julia had assumed it was just a form of graciousness, creating the illusion of a restaurant, of a better life. But the man says, "They aren't allowed to take food directly from the table. State health law. They can only touch what they have on their own plates. Might have picked up anything on the streets. Germs. Viruses. You know. But don't worry. They know the rules. They'll just tell you what they want."

Anthony shakes his head back and forth so quickly that Julia is afraid he might shake it off his shoulders. Were it not for him, she would hang back herself, perhaps leave altogether, mumbling about the absurdities of all social life, heading for her study, her books, with a determination born of falsely alleviated guilt. The world can go to hell, she might have muttered out loud as she flagged a cab uptown. But she is his mother. If she fails to set an example of fortitude, who will? So she nudges Anthony, leading him to a table where three people sit, hands folded before them. "Would you like cookies or doughnuts, coffee or tea?" she asks them, a born waiter.

"Both," answers the old white man who had shouted at them for staring at the sheet folding. His hands are rough and thick and clean. His eyes convey a burdensome clarity as he stares into the air before him. "Coffee for me, please. Tea for my wife." He lifts his chin in the direction of a bedraggled woman next to him. Her dyed red hair is knotted and wispy, her skin caked with several layers of pink powder that cracks in places, exposing narrow rivulets of tan flesh.

"Tea," she repeats, her eyes fixed on a dusty ball of green yarn she clutches in her hands.

"Anthony, they would like cookies and doughnuts. This is my son, Anthony," Julia tells them.

Briefly, the man looks surprised, noticing, Julia knows, her son's dark skin. She is used to this double take when she introduces her children. Even when they were very young and exactly the same olive tan as she is, people always knew. Their eyes would dart back and forth in an instant of surprise followed by a hostile or an overly friendly greeting. Julia feels a moment of mean gratification that the homeless man is white and will be served by a young black boy. But the man recovers and shakes Anthony's hand, muttering, "McNeil."

She moves over to the next person, inquiring about menu, while Anthony gathers the food. Finally, they are all seated at the table—Mr. and Mrs. McNeil, Anthony and Julia, and a middle-aged black man who has ordered doughnuts and tea.

"My name is Julia," she says to him, "and this is my son, Anthony."

"Weber," he tells them. "Welcome."

Mrs. McNeil throws her soiled yarn onto the floor and calls, "Cloudy, cloudy, cloudy." The yarn unravels for several feet and stops.

"Came up from Florida two years ago," her husband intones, as if it is habitual—this tiresome need to explain his wife's behavior. "Sold everything down there." He holds out a plate which Anthony instantly grabs and fills. "Had a cat up here named Cloudy."

74

"My cat's name is Pepper," Anthony says, and Julia is touched by his need, his effort to converse, but Mr. McNeil ignores him. Perhaps because he has to get the story out in order to avoid annoying questions, thinks Julia. She hopes it is not because Anthony is black.

"Then things got bad," he continues. "I lost my job. She needed an operation. We were evicted. Held on to Cloudy for a while on the streets, but in the end we lost her. Who knows? Maybe she found her way back to the apartment." He shrugs narrow, rounded shoulders. "Cats do that." He turns his head slightly in the direction of his wife. "She thinks it's still here."

"That's terrible," says Anthony, sounding so alarmed that Mr. McNeil finally smiles at him and asks, "Where do you go to school, son?"

While Anthony begins describing his private school, trying to slide over the location in the tree-lined streets of Riverdale, the huge playing fields, although Mr. McNeil is clearly interested in sports and perks up at the mention of Anthony's participation on the teams, Julia turns to Mr. Weber. As if resigned that it is his turn to speak, as if she is an elementary school teacher welcoming a new class, he says, "I'm from D.C. originally. Lived in Brooklyn for a while." And although his tone is conversational and without any resentment, this time color makes her feel ashamed of herself, a white woman requiring an older, poorer black man to tell his story.

"I come here with my wife," he says, nodding in the direction of a small, dark woman still engaged in preparing her belongings for the night. She takes a blue bathrobe from her shopping bag, folds it in her lap, then pulls one out for her husband and lays it across the pillow which she fluffs up before turning down the sheet. Carrying two white towels and a large plastic bag filled with soaps and creams, she walks out of the room as if she is alone and busy in her own home, as if there are not a dozen people seated at tables, many of them watching her intimate preparations for the night. As Julia, too, watches she thinks of her father, who died before Anthony was born, and who gave her one of her first lessons, she realizes now, in the uses of fiction.

"When you get old," he had told her one afternoon as they sat across from each other in his dingy kitchen eating herring on rye, "if you are living alone and are not entirely happy"—he winked and smiled ironically—"always set the table when you eat. Make your bed every day. And change your sheets once a week. A nice meal. A made bed. Clean sheets . . . it helps you stay on the straight path," he had said, clicking his tongue, indicating significance.

Then she remembers the previous time she'd remembered his advice. When her children were small and the apartment was filled with unpredictable paraphernalia and useless items (once she'd found seven used-up Scotch tape dispensers taking up room in a kitchen drawer); when dusty pennies rolled under every piece of furniture and discarded clothing remained stuffed in shopping bags for years, shoved into teeming closets; during those many years of mothering boys, when she often awoke in a panic fearful that her sanity would scatter before she could get them dressed, fed, and on their way to nursery school, herself to work and chores, especially then, she needed her old furniture precisely placed in a room, clean towels lined up on a rack for bath time, little shirts and jeans carefully folded in a drawer. Even a superficial orderliness had provided a bastion against the chaos threatening her self-control.

While Anthony begins including Mr. Weber in his discussion with Mr. McNeil about high school athletics, Mrs. Weber returns from her bath, a towel wrapped around her hair. She wears the blue robe, tied at the waist, furry slippers, and carries her clothing over her arm. She retrieves a book from her shopping bag and places it on her pillow, packs her folded clothing into the bag, and comes over to the table. Politely and firmly she instructs Anthony to bring her two doughnuts, four cookies, and one cup of hot tea with milk.

Julia goes to get her own cup of tea with milk, then returns to the table where she sits across from Mrs. Weber. But she cannot think of anything to say because she is overcome with an embarrassing fear. She is afraid that one day she too may be coming to a synagogue or church for shelter, left without a home when her children are grown and Bruce is who knows where. And she is embarrassed because here she is fearing for herself what has already happened to someone else. Anthony is only thirteen, but Daniel is in his last year of high school and will soon be gone. And it has always seemed, at times, a precarious fiction to her, this *family*—this being a mother—this sense of protection from the world and the coldness of its nights. She will always be a mother. She knows this. Until she is dead she will be a mother. Even after she is dead the motherness of her will remain in Daniel's and Anthony's minds. But being a mother of young children—that story is nearing its end, she thinks, watching Anthony, now completely engrossed in his conversation with Mr. Weber and Mr. McNeil. That true-to-life story, that collection of innumerable stories, is nearly finished, she thinks, and she pretends to have to go to the bathroom so no one will notice the tears in her eyes.

The bathroom is immaculate and smells of ammonia. Now that she's here she might as well pee, and when she's done she washes her hands. Standing over the sink, feeling the cool water on her wrists, she remembers how when she was a child she hated anyone to tell her what to do. Even sensible rules seemed offensive to her, so when her grandmother, who lived with them for some years, insisted that she wash her hands every time she went to the bathroom, she would instead let water run into the sink in case her grandmother was listening, but she would not wash her hands. Then, once, when the boys were small and Bruce's mother, an extravagantly clean woman, was spending many evenings with them, she found herself doing the same thing—going to the bathroom to pee, then letting the water run without washing her hands, feeling the same enjoyable edge of rebelliousness she'd felt as a child. Homeless, the need for shelter would subject you to all sorts of rules, and for someone like her—Daniel, for instance—too many rules of any kind could drive you mad.

She thinks about her cousin, a boy she'd been close to as a child, who had become a drug addict and eventually landed in jail. In one letter to her he'd said that the only way he could break their rules was by constructing even more rigid ones for himself—waking at five A.M., for instance, instead of the required six. And only in breaking their rules could he retain some sense of himself. Now, standing in the bathroom and feeling nearly sick from the ammonia smell, she feels as potentially alone as she has ever before felt, and the potential seems as painful as the fact might someday be. Or, perhaps it is not loneliness she feels, but what she imagines to be Mrs. Weber's despair which must surely lie beneath her stoical fictions involving habits of cleanliness and order. Or, Julia thinks while drying her hands on a rough paper towel, she is experiencing the more naked desperation of Mrs. McNeil. Yes, she is sure of it. She would fail to manage the small rescues devised by her father and Mrs. Weber. She would be unable to conjure up a belief that any of it mattered. Like Mrs. McNeil, she would go mad. But what if this is the self-indulgence black people and poor people often speak of, this presumption of knowledge, this insistence on imagining a suffering one has in fact always been spared? But no, she thinks, it is not the physical fact of homelessness and its implications she is claiming to feel. (Though she insists she can imagine that. Not that she can imagine any deprivation. But almost certainly this one.) It is the obvious fragility she suddenly perceives in all the stories she makes up and has made up about her life. The one, for instance, about how her children will never really leave her, even though they have (naturally) been slowly doing exactly that since the day they were born.

Once, years before, they had taken the boys south to visit Bruce's family. They had stayed on a large farm, the only land owned by either side of the family, where they grew tobacco and corn, raised and smoked pigs. There were three houses on the land in which three generations of Courtney Joneses lived—the old grandfather; the father, who lived in the big house and ran the farm; and one of the sons, about ten years younger than Bruce, a young man who was on his way up in the bank. The week Julia and her family were there, the dog had recently given birth to seven pups, just old enough to start tumbling and running around. Anthony, who had always loved animals (which is why they finally got him Pepper, although Bruce hates and fears cats), spent much of his time rolling around in the grass and mud with those puppies. He had always been a very active child, not really overactive in the clinical sense, the pediatrician told them, but almost. But here, he seemed normal, running all day and wrestling with puppies. There is a photograph framed on her bookcase at home—a large mountain of seven pups and Anthony climbing on top of each other, Anthony's face being licked by three pups at once. He seemed more at home on that southern farm he'd never before visited than he'd ever been in their city apartment where in moments, hours, of overactive energy, he crashed into walls, broke dishes, wrestled with Daniel until their giggles and screams, ordinary boyish shouting, nearly drove her mad. "Stop it!" she'd shout. "And right this minute." So that when Daniel, with his fast talking, got older, he'd subject her to lectures on the normality of brothers wrestling, shouting, even punching each other until one of them began to cry. "It's an oppression to us," he'd told her when he was a five-foot-ten-inch twelve-year-old and Anthony a lanky, clumsy eight. "Your need for silence."

They'd launch their large frames onto beds leaving broken springs in their wake. They broke chairs, closet doors hanging off admittedly sloppily constructed hinges. Once a window was shattered when Anthony threw a baseball at Daniel's head. And Daniel was right. It was the thundering sound of bodies rolling across the floor, the sudden screams and not the marred furniture that pushed her to the edge. "We *are* boys, you know," Daniel would accuse, ceasing their play, obedient and furious. "Can't you ever leave us alone?"

Though he was only thirteen, Daniel drove a tractor across the roads of the farm. He leaned forward in the driver's seat, steering the huge machine down dirt lanes, swerving for dogs and pigs. She watched in horror, but Bruce, made brave and cruel by his extended kin, joined all the Courtney Joneses in laughing at her. "Nothing can happen," they chuckled. "Leave the boy alone." Eventually, not to subject herself to further humiliation by conforming so predictably to the expectations of her gender, she retreated to the kitchen where the women were snapping beans.

"Those tractors," Aunt Bernice crooned when Julia sat down at the gleaming white Formica table and grabbed a bowl of garden vegetables to cut. "My boys loved 'em, too. Don't worry, honey," she said.

"Why shouldn't she worry?" said Bruce's cousin Laverne who had moved up to Washington and was down home for a visit, like Julia herself. "Courtney junior crashed one once and broke his leg. Don't you remember?"

"Oh, most of the time nothing happens," said Bernice, and turned back to her sink.

The next morning, Daniel began calling Julia "Mama" in the southern way, and his inflection was so perfect she felt a stranger to the name whose echoes of security and slavery she'd come to bless and curse. "Hey, Mama," he'd shout as the tractor swerved and tilted over dangerous hills. Anthony rushed over to her every so often and patted her back, saying, "Don't worry, Mom"—the name she knew—assuring her of her place before he bolted again.

"This is your home," she always told them periodically, but after they came home from the visit south she told them frequently for some time. "You can say anything you want here," she would repeat emphatically, drawing a contrast between home, the one created by her, and the world of schools (and southern farms) where a word like fuck, for instance, was forbidden, where children were expected to be polite rather than honest. This is what she thought she had to give—a tolerance for truth, for honest words. With the compulsion of religious faith in the literal Word of God, she had believed in the power of language to control life and protect love. As if there were no danger beyond their walls an honest declaration of feeling could not neutralize. As if there were no experience on earth she did not have the obligation and the endurance to describe.

She checks her watch, nervous that Anthony might be wondering where she is and eager for it to be time to go home. When she returns to the dining area, Mrs. McNeil is again calling out for Cloudy. Anthony is deep in conversation with Mr. Weber about the possibility of a Yankee-Met World Series, much as he might have been with Bruce. For another hour, Julia walks up and down the aisles, between tables, serving coffee and tea, speaking respectfully of superficial matters to as many people as she can. Then the volunteers who are sleeping overnight begin setting up their cots, and Anthony and Julia get ready to leave.

Mrs. Weber, who has been stacking the paper plates as if they are bone china, puts a restraining hand on Julia's arm. "He's a good boy," she says. "Be thankful he's a good boy." Julia is not sure if Mrs. Weber is addressing her with a welcoming intimacy as if Julia were black, or if she is instructing her about her son because she is white and might be too dumb to notice his nature. But she nods, feeling grateful and strangely relieved. Then Mrs. Weber turns to Anthony. "You keep being a good boy, hear?" she warns, managing to imply by her injunctions to them both the paradoxical belief that Julia has been blessed by fate in her son's essential goodness and that he must continue to exert a determined will against badness lurking at every corner of the dangerous streets. As soon as the situation is named with such clarity, Julia knows it is how she has been feeling all along. Then, as if she were going home, Mrs. Weber shakes both their hands and returns to her readied cot and her book. She turns her back to them and they are gone.

In the taxi, Anthony remains silent. Sleet falls harshly against the window panes. The car has no shock absorbers, so they bump up and down, falling against each other continually. "I was just thinking," he says at last, then looks away from her, out the side window.

"What?"

"I was wishing I could find their cat for them. I would go to the old neighborhood and find the house. Their old apartment would be dark and empty, but I'd hear the cat mewing, so I'd creep in, with a flashlight. Then I'd see Cloudy in a corner. They say cats can find their old homes, so she did. She was hungry and mangy. But she was still alive at least. I'd take her home and feed her until she was all well. Then I'd go back to the shelter one night and find Mr. and Mrs. Weber and give the cat back to them."

They enter the park road, twisting around curves. Passing headlights illuminate the angular structure of his face, creating white streaks on his brown skin. "Anthony," she says to him, placing a tentative hand on his thigh, "the cat belonged to Mr. and Mrs. McNeil. Remember? It wasn't the Webers."

"I know," he says. "But I was thinking about finding Cloudy, and I really liked the Webers. Not that I didn't like Mr. McNeil, though she was pretty weird. . . . But the Webers seemed so normal, like—like they could be my family. And I don't mean to hurt your feelings, Mom, but I am black, you know."

So here, as if she were writing a story, is the clarity she hadn't planned on. Besides the desire to help Anthony manage his empathy for the world, her own need to do something to help, she was constructing a story she could live by: about working in a homeless shelter, but also one about the closeness of a mother and a son, a story implying that no matter how separate they must learn to be, they are still—well, *one* in a way, different yet the same. Here is the danger, and apparently it stalks her whether or not she writes the stories down. Because now she is silent in the taxi as Anthony relives aloud the details of the past three hours. "Did you see how Mrs. Weber acted as if she were in her own house? Did you hear how much Mr. Weber knew about sports? He was like a walking encyclopedia, Mom. It's incredible. How did that happen to them? I mean losing their home . . ." But as he goes on she hears only the timbre of his voice and behind the voice the rhythmic beat of sleet against the window, the *whoosh* of cars speeding by them. Then all the sounds meld into one low backup to the voice she hears in her head.

What color am I, Mom?

Anthony was a lithe and slender child, and she ran admiring fingers across his narrow ribs, down his bumpy spine. His hair, brown like hers, caught gold and red in the light. Daniel was thick in the shoulders, like Bruce, but his thighs were slightly too short for his torso, like Julia's. His nose was small, like hers, and his mouth might have been a carefully designed replica of her mother's.

83

What color am I, Mom?

Perhaps gold, or bronze, she thought, studying their flesh.

It is 1981, and Daniel is graduating from the sixth grade. Along with all the other parents, she sits in the auditorium, waving the program across her face to make the air move. Strains of music begin, a trill of scales, then the two chords she recalls from her own elementary school days that mean "Stand up." They stand, along with all the fifth-, fourth-, and third-graders attending the ceremony. Now "Pomp and Circumstance" fills the room. A few fathers move into the aisle, kneeling, cameras ready to snap when their child marches in. Girls in organdy and pique. Boys in dark pants, white shirts, and red-and-blue ties around such thin and insubstantial necks. There are faces of pale tan and pink (what she used to call flesh color in her crayon drawings when she was a child), faces of olive brown, faces of tan with an ocher tint in this neighborhood famous for its ethnic complexity. The line of girls passes down one aisle, boys down the other, all walking in time to the music, smiling, size places. Now the tallest boys come down the aisle, the end of the line, and for the most part their faces are dark brown, half a dozen shades from burnt sienna to nearly black. The black boys are in the back of the line, most of them the tallest ones in the sixth grade. But there in their midst is Daniel, brown flesh sparkling, dark curls reaching around his shell-like ears.

"What color am I, Mom? I mean, what *color* am I? Not what color am I *really*. You know what I mean. What *color* am I? Really. Am I black? Like Daddy?"

"You are black like Daddy," she says.

And now, as he walks past her with the tallest boys, she sees that he is.

For weeks after that night, the walls of their apartment are permeable to the Webers and the McNeils. They worry

84

about them in late night rainstorms that before would have increased the warm comfort of their beds. Julia makes up stories for Anthony of happier endings so he can fall asleep, and somehow, although he knows they are not true, he feels temporarily comforted. Then she returns to her bed and unrestful sleep, dreaming of dangerous streets that mock her fictions of fairness and control. She finds she is unable to describe the shelter in her journal but to record the memory of that night can manage only this: Speeding down the winding park road, surrounded by passing shadows that may be men and women huddled under plastic garbage bag tents, in the dark interior of the taxi I am stark white and visible.

Black and Blue

What did I do
To be so black and blue?

—*Louis Armstrong*

Each time, he thinks of his father never finishing high school, then remembers his own crumbling, poorly equipped schoolhouse. Each time, she thinks of her father leaving school in the fifth grade to learn the skills of a weaver.

Red and gray stone buildings border a shady quad. A winding path leads to the playing fields. It is late October, and the numerous trees are heavy with purple and yellow leaves. Each time they come here for a parents' meeting, one of them says, I'm glad we send them here. Even though we had to sacrifice. Even though it compromises our principles. At least they can see the seasons change. At least they are safe here. At least there are other black kids in this private school.

But often in class, Anthony or Daniel will tell them, there is no other black kid. And that can be hard, Anthony once said. How? she asked, fully attentive. How exactly?

—Well, take my English class this week, he answered. We were discussing whether novels can be racist, and all the other kids said they can't because art just shows how the world is and doesn't take a position. And besides, if the book is a great one for lots of reasons, why talk about its racism? So I told them about that line I found in

Hemingway, and even Whitman slips once and calls us "the heavy lipped slave." Anthony's eyelids close slightly as they do when he is in pain. —But this writer, Penn Warren, keeps using *nigger* and *nigger woman,* and his black characters are always saying shit like "Lawd God, hit's a-nudder one done done hit." Well, I definitely think it's racist. But when I say that the whole class is against me. They laugh at me, a kind of scornful laugh. And the teacher too.

—The teacher too?

—Well, she doesn't laugh but she says it's not relevant that these writers can seem racist today. It was normal for their times.

Daniel snorts. Bruce says, Shit. Julia says, Normal for who?

In his English class this semester there are no other black kids besides Daniel. And so on Parents' Day, when mothers and fathers crowd the classrooms to observe, Daniel and Bruce are the only black people in the room. The class is reading the novel *Invisible Man,* and the teacher, a man Julia trusts, smiles at them all with a trick-ster face, about to lead them through labyrinths and around edges of pits they cannot yet imagine. His blue eyes twinkle. He leans against the blackboard and puts his hands in his pockets. He begins to talk about the color imagery in the novel, black and white mixing, colliding, contrasting. Red splashing over white, even in the first few pages, the red liquid of sloe gin dripping over the white mound of ice cream. The students realize right away it's blood imagery. Then they talk about color, how they see color in their lives, how they see color on other skin. Daniel is silent. Bruce smiles slightly with one side of his mouth. He twists his pencil around and around in his hand.

They have all read the "Prologue" in which the name-less narrator asserts his invisibility, curses and claims it,

88

then describes hundreds of lights he has hung in his stolen basement room, lighting up his world, his face, as he listens to music.

—Let's talk a bit, then I'll play you the song he's listening to in this chapter, says Mr. Sonelle with an impish grin.

There is a tape player on one of the empty front desks. Slowly, Mr. Sonelle inserts the tape but doesn't turn it on. Julia herself has just taught this novel to her college class. She has taught it because of the intricacies of its imagery, because of its place in American history, because it reminds her so intensely of how it is to feel invisible. She elbows Bruce who hasn't read the novel in ten years and has forgotten—she can see by his quizzical look— what is coming next. Daniel, she thinks, has never heard the song. He looks down at his notebook, tracing doodles with his pen. He has completed over half the book already, ahead of the class, but he is the only black student in the room, and he looks down, doodling.

Julia feels the familiar dislocation of her now lifelong double consciousness. She remembers twenty years before, the first time she was sent out to get a cab for Bruce with a white woman's confidence, he appearing only after the cab had come to a full stop. She hears Daniel's four-year-old voice coming in from play, asking—What's a nigger, Mom? She is black inside, she thinks with an ironic smile which Mr. Sonelle notices and returns. He is about to undermine the illusions of these well-meaning white children who would say, if asked, that there is no difference, we are all the same, what matters is what you are inside.

Which she too would have said (and would still say), as she was raised by radical, immigrant Jews to believe that "Negroes are the same as everyone else." But the sentence never reads the other way around.

She has also learned with her children's developing consciousness that black people know it is never the same.

And so, the other night, Saturday, when she and Bruce were alone in the house (Anthony sleeping over at a friend's, Daniel out for the evening) and he told her what his administrative assistant, a young white man, asked him the other day, she knew his answer before he finished the story. But she wanted him to tell her, so she remained silent. Anyway, they have three hours to wait in the unsatisfying half sleep of Saturday nights, the restless dozing to which they have become accustomed since Daniel began staying out well past midnight. She is afraid of muggers, of cabs passing him by until streets are deserted, that he will drink too much. And now Bruce has taught her to fear the police who will see not *Daniel* but a black boy out for a night on the town.

They set the clock for two, but she tries to remain awake anyway, because she is afraid that she will wake up to the alarm, find Daniel not home and be frightened out of her mind. To avoid that possible moment of fear, which is unrealistic since Daniel is always on time, she keeps her eyes opened and tries, through extending conversation any way she can, to keep Bruce awake too. He tries to stay awake with her because he knows she wants him to, but he resents it because if left to his own desires he would certainly go to sleep. Daniel is seventeen. He will be leaving home soon. Even Anthony will begin going out at night by the end of the year. What's he supposed to do? Never get any sleep on Saturday night? Every time his eyelids droop, he jerks himself awake and sees her watching him.

—Then let's sit up and read, he says, annoyed. I hate this in-between shit.

It is incomprehensible to him, her need to keep a pointless vigil. As if her consciousness will somehow protect them from the harm of the streets.

The television is on, a low background noise. They are reading the Sunday papers. She lies in bed. He sits in the old armchair from her father's house, its white linen cover beginning to tear. Underneath the slipcover, Julia has patched the torn upholstery with layers of carpet tape that is partially visible, silver and frayed. The house is weirdly and pleasantly quiet when the boys aren't home. Since he has to stay up, he might as well tell her the story of how Phil, his administrative assistant, asked him that question the other day. She will like the story because she likes him to tell her about his life, which he rarely does, and because the end of the story is how he suddenly, unexpectedly cried. She will like that he cried.

—I had this experience yesterday, he says, lifting his eyes from *The News of the Week in Review,* and she instantly takes off her glasses, excited, a childlike attention that still, after all these years, charms him.

—You know Phil? My assistant? We were sitting in the office, and it was a slow day. We were talking about politics and all of a sudden he says to me: What was the hardest thing about growing up black in the south during segregation?

Bruce is fond of Phil, but he is no closer to him than he is to most people. Not *close* as she meant the word. Not in the sense that he'd bring him home for dinner. He almost never brings his friends home for dinner, Daniel reminds him accusingly. It's hard for him to understand Julia's and Daniel's need for friends. One of them is always on the phone with someone, talking for hours, planning or getting ready for or returning from "dates."

—Can't he ever be by himself? Bruce complained to Julia one night after they'd recovered from the usual ten or twelve calls.

—They're his friends, she answered defensively, as if he had criticized her. He needs to talk to them. You wouldn't understand.

Along with their ardent attachment to each other, there is this stream of never-ending conflict. Her wanting him to be something he never can be. He feels bruised by all the years of it. And recently, she had said, pleased with her beloved double meanings, Oh, I'm just sore from it all, Bruce. Don't talk to me about anything. That'll be just fine.

But he sees the fairness of her need for a sort of companionship he finds hard to provide. His solitariness gets in the way. It has been with him always. He has never known himself to be any other way.

He remembers sitting on the porch at home, the town quiet, nothing happening by seven o'clock in the evening and all day Saturday and Sunday, quiet as death. In this idea of *nothing happening* he includes the visits of neighbors, always talking about the same things, his family arguing incessantly. On the other hand, one was always subject to the most annoying intrusions. Everyone thought they knew you, that they had a right to tell you who you were. And there must have been other things that made him hate the memory of that town, the sorts of things he might not mention to his black friends, fearing they would misunderstand. They would accuse him of undervaluing his Blackness, question his commitment. He had started his working life as a neighborhood organizer, then as a lawyer and government official in the human services (which always meant services for those humans too poor to buy them). Still, people are uncomfortable when you are different from them. He remembers sitting on the porch, smelling whatever his mother was cooking for dinner, nodding politely to whichever visitors were coming to talk, watching his older brother signifying and hand slapping with the other guys, and he would think: I am going to get out of here. He had thought it since he was about six years old: the small-townness of it; the repetitiveness, like slow-motion movements in a dull, predictable dance. The way people were always in your business, thought they knew you, thought they had the right to tell you who you were.

—But you seem pretty happy whenever we go down there, Julia told him, enjoying the opportunity of pointing out layers of contradiction Bruce preferred to ignore. —Yeah, how about that time with Anthony and the puppies? Daniel piped up. Lately, he and Anthony had been wanting to go south more often, for holidays and vacations. It's our heritage, Dad, Anthony said to him recently. Bruce sighed.

When Phil asked him the question, Bruce thought about it seriously, laying his pen down.

Good or bad, almost all of his childhood memories are connected with race in a way that white people's memories never would be. He remembers the black project he lived in, the black school he attended, the white swimming pool he could not swim in even though he was black state champion.

—So what did you say? she asks, sitting up in bed. She already knows what he will say, something about the artificial limits on his life, perceived so young, the lack of possibilities.

At times he feels as if he can hear her thoughts, and it was not only the twenty years of living together that made it so. He'd felt it from the beginning, that somehow he knew what she was feeling because she was who he might have been if he had been someone else. Which does not mean he always likes what he sees. He worries about Anthony, who is overly sensitive. Until his tenth year he played with dolls, then hid them when friends came over to the house. Every other week he had something wrong with his stomach, or his head ached. Until he was thirteen, she kept a mattress in their room for him since he had nightmares nearly every night and couldn't get back to sleep alone. —Isn't he a little old for this, Bruce would hiss at her in the dark. —At least we can all go to sleep, she'd say, hiding her own happiness in providing this comfort for Anthony.

Julia told Bruce once that he should be able to understand; once he must have been like that, was therefore still like that down deep. —Maybe I was long ago, he'd told her sadly, but not now. It's long gone. Believe me.

—What about that time last June when we heard the Vietnamese woman talk about her experience being a boat person? Julia countered, wanting him to identify with Anthony. You were crying, remember? Not everyone was, but you were.

—It was early in the morning, he had told her. I always cry if something sad happens early in the morning.

—There's nothing wrong with indulging them a little, she'd said, insisting on the mattress for Anthony.

She could never understand, he had thought, the distance he'd travelled, his own sort of boat-person life, moving from one world to another of a completely different kind. When she expressed every feeling that crossed her brain, it frightened him. It seems right to him, what he learned as a child—that you have to harden yourself to some degree. There has to be some callous, numb part. When he ignores her feelings, or criticizes her for the intensity of her reactions or for paying too much attention to Anthony's, it is not that he does not, "will never as long as he lives and breathes" (she says) understand. It is that he feels angered by what he sees. She senses this and accuses him of coldness. But the word is wrong, and once, when he was feeling apologetic and ashamed, he gave her the right word: callous. I can be callous, he warned her, looking sadly into her eyes.

In Daniel's English class, Mr. Sonelle is asking the students what they make of the violence of the "Prologue": *I pulled his chin down sharp upon the crown of my head, butting him as I had seen the West Indians do and I felt the flesh tear and blood gush out . . . I kicked him repeatedly in a frenzy . . . and in my outrage I got out my knife and prepared to slit his throat . . .* The teacher reads the words aloud slowly. Is this rage extreme? he asks.

—It sure seems extreme to me, a girl says.

94

—It's not extreme, someone else argues. The guy called him a nigger, or we're made to believe he did. He's probably heard it all his life. He just exploded. He lives in this dark world where no one really sees him.

—But if the guy called him a nigger, he saw him, didn't he? So why does he keep saying he's invisible? Mr. Sonelle asks.

The week before, Julia had attended a poetry reading in her school given by ten students, six white, four black. The white students wrote about lots of things, she told Anthony the next evening as he rummaged through the refrigerator looking for snacks. But all four black students wrote about being black. Why is that?

—For them, everything is related to race, her son told her.

—Is it for you? she asked. And for some reason, said it again—Is it for you?

—Well, yes, he said. I know it's the first thing people see about me wherever I go. White people, I mean. They don't think, There's a boy. They think, There's a black boy. I'm very aware of that. I'm always black, so they never see *me*. He strikes his chest hard with a fist which she feels against her temple, then, as if to take her breath away, against her heart.

Mr. Sonelle is waiting for someone to answer his question. He leans against the blackboard, looks at the ceiling, contented with the nervous silence in the room. Finally Daniel says—Because they don't see him. They only see his blackness. But he keeps his eyes on his notebook where he continues doodling. Now Bruce is looking down too, and Julia feels her skin is scorched by their blackness, like a branding iron would scorch her skin. Her skin seems to go up in smoke from a body that is hot, wounded.

Mr. Sonelle nods at Daniel, then looks at the rest of the students, eyebrows raised. She is wondering, as she has at other times like this—somewhere at the edge of her mind there is a sense of turmoil—if Bruce ever regrets being married to her, a white woman.

But he thinks of her more as a Jewish woman than simply a white woman. Not that the Jews in the town where he grew up were that much better than other whites, but once he moved to New York it was obvious that some Jews maintained an assiduous sensitivity to any oppression. Her father had been such a Jew, an immigrant from a small town in Romania, and Bruce had come to love him. He'd spent one summer nursing him back to health after a heart attack. Julia, pregnant with Daniel and in graduate school, was away from the apartment at dinnertime when the anxiety and loneliness that brought on her father's heart attack in the first place threatened to engulf him with the coming of the dark. Bruce wasn't sure what he made of such psychosomatic interpretations—his father-in-law had nothing but disdain for them—but Julia believed in them thoroughly at the time. (Now, Bruce realizes this belief backfires upon her with cruel irony. Now that one of her children is ill, she has to fight every day against the belief that the illness is rooted in personality and—since all the mothers he knows seem to believe they are the cause of everything about their children and live with a constant self-aggrandizing, self-immolating guilt—that it is therefore her fault.) Sam smoked two packs of cigarettes a day. Like most Jews of his generation, physical exercise was, to him, something admirable and slightly incomprehensible, something gentile. A heart attack was a heart attack, Bruce tended to believe along with his father-in-law. But even the doctor had suggested a psychological element in this case.

During the summer, Bruce would return from his job at five-thirty and begin to make dinner for the two of them. He didn't know how to cook, but between Sam's haphazard instructions and Julia's detailed recipes, he learned. And he discovered a surprising pleasure in food preparation—cutting vegetables, learning about spices and the wonderful variety of mustards, an even greater pleasure in serving food to an appreciative diner, in this case one whose life depended on it—especially if Julia's and the doctor's theory was to be believed. It was the pleasure of these activities that converted Bruce, as much as the obvious fairness of the arguments of the then incipient women's movement, to become a highly competent housekeeper. Even now, twenty years later when Sam was fifteen years dead, Bruce could hear his voice praising him almost every evening at dinner: *Excellent, son, excellent.* Or, *Not as good as last night,* Sam told him once, *but not bad.* Bruce enjoyed the honest evaluations, being called Son, the silent knowledge between them of traveling from one sort of world to another; what you lost along the way.

Mr. Sonelle is trying to get the white students to hear what Daniel has said to them, to comprehend it so they will understand the novel and the terrible lyrics of the song Louis Armstrong is about to sing. How can you get people who have never experienced such things to understand that the world can twist the self, spin it into hideous distortions until it turns around to punish the world? How do you crack the sense of entitlement wide enough to teach that behind and within every fiction is the story of a real life? —Why read this book? Mr. Sonelle asks. —Why read any book?

—So tell me, she insists again, wanting to hear the story about Phil exactly as it happened. But just then the cat jumps onto the bed and stretches on Bruce's pillow. Bruce sneezes. —We have to get rid of this damn cat, he says. I hate this cat. —You're afraid of it, admit it, Anthony had shouted at him. But Bruce himself had gone with Anthony to Bide-a-Wee to get the cat nearly eight years before. —I should never have done it, he says now.

—Why did you? she asks. Why didn't you say no?

—Everyone wanted it, Bruce says. You all made me feel so guilty.

She remembers other times when Bruce's failure to insist on what he wants makes him angry at them for weeks. —You think you were being kind, she accuses.

—Not kind, he says. It's that I don't have any right.

—What did you say to Phil? she asks again. You didn't finish your story.

—Well, I tried to remember, he says, leaning back in the old chair. —It all started coming back to me, how I felt growing up there, and how happy I was when I came to New York. He points his toes toward each other, chews on the frame of his glasses, smiles when he thinks of the city. Even now, with the housing crisis, the mental health crisis, the employment crisis, the crime crisis, even though they sit home every Saturday night after midnight and wait anxiously for Daniel and soon Anthony (if Julia weren't there, he'd probably remain half-awake, keeping an eye on the clock until two)—still, he can walk through the city streets and feel the excitement of first arriving here twenty-five years before. It was a new world, and even after all these years parts of it remain new, unknown to him. It fills him with a sense of possibility, there being always something unknown. He likes what is distinct from his own life—new foods, new places, new sorts of people. It was Julia's difference he was drawn to, that she wasn't numbed (though he wishes she were at times); that she was a writer (though now she hasn't written in years).

—I hated that town, he says. But it wasn't only the town itself, of course. So I said to Phil —The hardest thing was the sense of restricted possibility, that from so young an age, maybe five or six, you knew you would never be all you could be.

But certainly he has told her this before, he worries now. His answer can't come as anything new to her. Then he sees real excitement in her eyes, some hidden pleasure he doesn't understand.

98

—"Only help her to know . . . that she is more than this dress on the ironing board, helpless before the iron," she says.

His brows knit in confusion.

—It's a line from Tillie Olsen, she tells him. The last line of a famous story. That's what the story's about, what you just said. "So all that is in her will not bloom—but in how many does it?"

He nods and smiles, feeling her happiness as their worlds meet. Here they were, she would be thinking now, exactly the same feeling at exactly the same moment, so rare for them.

In the release this feeling provides, she remembers old wounds, the insecurities of her childhood and his. Legacies of slavery and Eastern European poverty, generations of hardship coming to rest in their life, the first generation of precarious comfort, a startling expectation of safety she can suddenly feel. She remembers her father's chronic depression infiltrating every day of her childhood until she felt she carried it around in her flesh. The house always in disrepair, beyond his ability to cope, drawers clamped shut by garbage no one had gone through in years, cracked and useless dishes kept for decades under newer ones of plastic bought in a corner hardware store on sale. The paradox of his ability to inspire a union meeting to belief and action and his lifelong sense of strangeness in the world. "I need a comfortable chair," he had called them once to say. "What should I do?" Bruce had taken him to a furniture store two blocks away. She thinks of Bruce's mother who fights for every inch of what is owed to her, her children, her grandchildren, who plots with the brilliance of a fanatic and plans with the fastidiousness of a lawyer each time it seems the world may do her in. In her apartment are enough xerox copies of enough bills, letters and memos to stock a paper warehouse, along with every piece of furniture, sheet and towel she has ever owned, cluttering up the small space in case any member of the family, not yet on his or her feet, may get an apartment and need something. She is thinking of Daniel's conviction and belief in himself—how he would talk to anyone on the street when he was three years old, asking questions, expecting their interest. Of Anthony, weeping about the misery in the world yet whispering to her in the dark of burning self-confidence that somehow he will help to change things. *Warring races divided / yet inside of me / the two races beautifully united,* he has written in a recent poem. This belief in their power and goodness it took generations to make.

She leans back against the pillows. What has drawn us together? she is thinking: some reparation of old mistrust? of lack of faith? He had known the meaning of faith for the first time when he was in jail during the civil rights movement. It was only one night, he often says, but it was jail! Maybe we were singing, but it was jail! But in that night he felt something new. Not certainty of victory, nor fearlessness. But faith that something good existed. She had known the meaning first when she completed her first novel—the idea that she could do it; or it was when the children were born, after all that pain, Daniel and Anthony. But no, before that, it was Bruce. He sees that he is what she first knew of faith, his body, maternal, promising even what may be false to assuage the harshness of the moment, answering her whisper that yes, he will hold her when she is dying, he will forgive her her rages, her betrayals, her sadness, he will watch the clock with her. He remembers himself as a boy, surrounded by light (it seems to him now when he thinks of it), while visitors and even his family float transparently around him. He is sitting alone on the front porch until he has her, and Daniel, and Anthony.

—And before I knew what was happening, he says to her, I began to cry.

He had let so long a silence pass after she'd quoted him the lines from Tillie Olsen, she had returned to her paper, put her glasses back on. Perhaps he hadn't planned to tell her, or had forgotten, but now he wants her to know. She takes her glasses off again. Tears come to her eyes.

—Yes, he says, right there in front of Phil, a man I hardly know. I cried. I had to pretend I had to go to the bathroom so I could get away.

They are quiet together. She touches the soft curls of his hair.

—Do you ever regret that you married someone white? she says.

—Oh my God, he says. You're white?

The darkest, wordless interior of Armstrong's blues opens to her, resonates through the room, through their bodies. Daniel says, *Yeah!* nods his head emphatically, raises his eyes to Mr. Sonelle's giving him the thumbs-up sign. He looks back at his parents and sees her crying. He lowers his brows anxiously, shakes his finger at her, warning against any too obvious display of emotion. She shades her eyes with her hand since she can't control her tears. The lyrics sear into her. *I'm white inside, but that don't help my case. 'Cause I can't hide what is in my face.* Bruce winces—all the white people in the room who might misunderstand—brutal and poignant words fifty years ago that would never be used today. But the twisted meanings linger, layer into the sound of the trumpet, the dark heart of the blues not shrinking from the horror of this history, what I am not is good, what I am is bad, their terms, my terms, *wish'd I was dead.* Body shapes and flesh tones spin around her. As the music comes to a stop Bruce is tapping his pencil on the table to the final notes, and in the silence another tap, two, three. Then Mr. Sonelle's voice reading to them from the last pages of the novel: *but then I remind myself that true darkness lies within my own mind. . . . Still the passion persists. Sometimes I feel the need to reaffirm all of it, the whole unhappy territory and all the things loved and unlovable in it, for all of it is a part of me. Till now, however, this is as far as I've gotten, for all life seen from the hole of invisibility is absurd. So why do I write, torturing myself to put it down?*

She is thinking of generations of struggle for goodness, of Bruce's mother's mother, half-white like Daniel and Anthony. Really? Anthony said smiling broadly when he first heard this piece of his history. Really? He was so young, they didn't have the heart to tell him about the rapist great-grandfather, how that half-white daughter must have felt inside. She was like me, Anthony said. Her skin smokes, burns. *My only sin is in my skin.* She has silenced her own story with shame it cannot be too hard to name, not when she thinks of what others have named before. She is across a wide gulf speaking in a thundering whisper that is almost a shout, trying to bridge their differences with her voice.

TWO

~

Julia's Notebook

~

*What do I mean by alive? What I mean by alive—
not to shrink from what is most difficult: to
change one's image of oneself.*
> —Cassandra, *Christa Wolf*

*Ideally, the structure of the experience coincides
with the structure of the narrative. This should be
the goal: fantastic accuracy. But there is no tech-
nique that permits translating an incredibly tangled mesh, whose threads are interlaced according
to the strictest laws, into linear narrative without
doing it serious damage.*
> —Patterns of Childhood,
> *Christa Wolf*

~ A woman who writes/a woman who does not write.

A lifelong need for silence, suddenly ascendant. Certainly that.

A fear of exposure. No, that is what it was at first, immediately following the "traumatic event." Then it became an unwillingness to expose. Why, Martha said to me, are you willing to hurt me? It was a brilliantly constructed sentence.

Two stories, both mine, lead to the same moment in time, as if they were two stories about two different people from an older fiction—in Dickens, perhaps—told separately but moving toward a meeting, a clash, where they erupt into a third story, the real one being plotted all along: the story of Daniel, hardest of all to tell, the one I was able to avoid by making him a secondary character in the stories about Julia; and the story of Martha that lies beneath (perhaps even falsifies?) what has been told so far. Yet the real plot of this story is how a woman who loves words begins to love silence. No—even that is a metaphor, a layer over the core. The central story is about change, how difficult even the smallest change of character can be, how we hold on tenaciously to what we are, knowing that land and sea can shift unpredictably around even the most apparently innocuous transformation. Any novelist knows this—how hard it is to change someone without building up to it for pages. Just as it took me a decade to answer her question.

I might write an essay (instead of this compulsive record) on the uses of the self in fiction, the ethical as well as the aesthetic problems involved. Then I would construct a related piece on the limits of the self in motherhood, the terrible danger of false stories. I would keep the tone carefully abstract, avoiding the problem of character as well as exposure. But abstractions without the risk of detail are not the business of the fiction writer, and this notebook is a fiction in a way. Fiction, I am always reminding my students, is not a lie but a story, and the ability to see stories in experience along with the need to tell them is one way among many to get at the truth. There is no way to get there, however, by stating the generality: there is a road from here to there. You have to walk the road, find the turns, notice the grayness of the concrete speckled with dots of glistening mica chips, feel the weight of the wearying inclines and the ever-so-slight lightness of walking downhill.

Still, I resist this unmasking. I pile other books and projects on top of this journal and then pretend to have mislaid it for days. A treacherous voice in my head joins the chorus of contempt for certain kinds of women's autobiography. In my classes in autobiographical writing, for instance, the male students, even the shy ones, rush to self-revelation like young gods about to create the world in their image. They write of their mothers, who have been kind or incompetent, loving or neglectful. The fathers are gigantic. They sprawl and stomp across the pages of their sons' prose. Fathers whose brutality poisoned the childhoods of their little boys. Fathers whose vulnerable hearts beat like half-heard melodies through their sons' days, whose weakness broke their sons' hearts.

.

(He was hardly ever home—he drank, and when he drank he threw me against the wall—locked me in the closet—called me a queer—always took care of me after my mother left—met me for dinner and told me how much he loved me—wanted me to be a writer because that was his lost dream; he never said so, but I knew—and I could see the softness in his eyes / the pain of defeat in the way his shoulders rounded / once I saw him cry / I could see my own face reflected in his when I looked into his coffin . . .) *Dad!* I could hear the stark shout behind all the passionate prose. I had come to wait for it in the autobiographies of the boys, now called men in order to be fair, since the girls were now called women. They seemed to become men and women by the time they were juniors or seniors. At first, their boys' faces, with scratchy new beards, long braids, shaven heads, or purple-and-green spikes, seemed no more men's faces than the face of Daniel, or Anthony, nearly the same age as these sons, always rushing around trying to assume some kind of complex, elusive, changing, ill-fitting, appealing, and certainly almost always graceless manhood.

When women students write autobiography, they begin with some form of the words: Well, this is only my story / only personal / just what happened to me, but . . . Or they cannot begin at all because anything they might want to say seems to them to be so "self-indulgent." That is the word they use. I remember very well when it came into frequent use in reviews of women's work, in the early 1970s when women were writing so fiercely and so voluminously about themselves. "Self-indulgent" was the perfectly exact accusation, perfect for shaming females for whom goodness has been defined as indulging others. And the other word, equally stunning compound of effective construction: *self-involved.* (Just as her word had been perfect: *willing.* Why are you *willing* to hurt me?)

I fear the formlessness of this notebook because I am afraid of certain truths. Yet I need to know the truth with the sort of undeniable recognition that for me comes only with language. In all the stories I have constructed, paying careful attention to unity and shape, something has eluded me, some truth I am after, and I have seen that with all my controls, all my stories about control (though it was necessary for me to learn these things), I am in danger of creating a new mythology equally false to the old mythology of emotional spontaneity I lived by once, Daniel, when you were small.

"What is more important to you, Mommy? Me or your work?" you asked one night long ago as I rubbed your back and hummed *I'll be loving you always.* I was dumbstruck. I, who had never put my work before you, not in the sense that you would feel it? I had not gone away from home seeking solitude, teaching possibilities in other cities. I had hardly ever postponed dinner, for God's sake, because a chapter needed finishing. Still, I could not answer the question instantly, not at the time. (Now I know the answer perfectly well, the answer, at least, to the question you were asking. You, I would say now without hesitating.) "What a question!" was my evasive answer then. You, however—Daniel—are nothing if not persistent. "What is more important?" "Why do you ask?"— stalling for time. "Mom!" you yelled, threatening the peace of the night, the room straightened at last, the clean sheets I had put on the bed after washing the mattress clean of layers of urine (my fault, I knew, the anxiety I caused you), my rhythmic back rubbing, humming words of love—*not for just an hour, not for just a day, not for just a year, but always.* "I love you best," I finally said.

But I wasn't sure it was the truth. And you knew it, I feared, though perhaps you did not. Anyway, you fell asleep after I answered you. Before I fell asleep, I told myself this was another secret I could not tell, that my work, my self, my self-indulgent, self-involved self was more important to me than my son. I see now that what

I thought was a secret truth was really only a mask for a truth far more frightening: I would never again love anything, including myself, more than you and Anthony. Even now, confronting this notebook, this odd confession, I seek self-involvement as I once sought self-restraint, with equal desperation and doubt of attainment.

That night, I turned toward the window and watched the ripple of the bone white curtains curving into the room as they filled with wind. The bed was wide enough for me to feel as if I were alone, Bruce's body curved away from me. I watched a green candle burn in my favorite brass candlestick, the curtain sway with the wind, and my mind was eased by the simplicity of it. The delicate flame. The highlights of the brass below the dark candle. The bone white streaks of light on the curtains as cars passed below. The slight feel of the wind which had grown stronger and now blew the curtains more roughly into the room.

Why does this memory come to me now? Clearly, I am reminding myself of the depth of my love for you as the story threatens to become more explicit. These are the dangers of autobiography. It's not always the content of memories but their juxtaposition in which real meaning lies.

A woman who writes / a woman who does not write.

An out-of-control mother who adored her sons tried to gain, because of her passion for them, a capacity for control. For this woman, such an attempt meant one thing above all: she had to learn how to shut her mouth.

I always knew the time would come, right from the early days of Daniel's life when I found myself screaming at an infant in a carriage to go to sleep or I would lose my mind.

It is irrational, Daniel, who has a passionate belief in

reason, would say now, to think you can quiet a screaming infant by screaming at him. Indeed, it was.

But I had always defined myself by lack of control, feeling strong when I gave in to impulse, self-righteously
maintaining an explosive reaction to many things in life.
When I was a child, I talked all the time, and often louder
than was necessary. Moreover, I said things designed purposely to shock people, especially my elders, who were
so eminently and predictably shockable. *"Fuck Mrs. Ger-
ber!"* I would yell, for example, when my grandmother
warned me to be quieter in the halls, where good children
were supposed to be seen and not heard. And my grandmother would respond, "Shhh. It's a *shanda* for the
neighbors." Not knowing Yiddish, I thought she was
naming the loud and rebellious girl in me. It's *her* talking,
I thought my grandmother was saying to me each time I
shouted or lectured or disobeyed. It's Ashanda for the
neighbors. It's Ashanda talking for the neighbors. It's Ashanda controlling the world with her mouth, Ashanda
with her admonishments and lectures and stories and
words. Oh, Ashanda had conviction. Nothing if not that.
She'd tell you where to get off, where to get on, and what
it had been like. Telling you, she expected the world to
change. For instance, when she was eighteen, and her favorite uncle had become sick, she waited one night with
the rest of her family in the hospital praying for good
news. But secretly, Ashanda believed Uncle Freddie was
going to die. No matter how hard she tried to obey when
her aunt admonished them all to keep their hopes up, that
Freddie could feel the energy of their hope and it would
help him pull through, she couldn't stop this belief from
repeatedly entering her consciousness. That very night,
right before the sun came up, he died, and although the
doctors assured them all that nothing more could have
been done, Ashanda believed her thought had caused Uncle Freddie's death. She also believed if she wanted something with sufficient intensity—purity, she called it

(because if opposite thoughts came into her brain, the impact of the internal energy on external matters would be nullified)—that thing would be hers. So she began writing stories about Uncle Freddie, expecting to bring him back to life. And when he failed to materialize, she assumed she had not yet written the right story and began again.

Ashanda, most people agreed, was a little bit crazy. She had fits, for one thing, when she would thrash around the floor screaming unintelligibly, causing her father and her grandmother much anxiety. When she calmed down and one of them was soothing her, she'd tell them, "The thoughts were getting me," or, "I was hearing the voices," intensifying their concern even more. Sometimes she saw rats eat their way out of walls and fling themselves down on her bed, and she'd wake the whole house with her screaming. They took her to doctors. "Preschizophrenic reaction," said one. "Oversensitivity," another told them. "Too vivid an imagination, that's all it is," said a third. It wasn't that she saw a rat eating out of the wall and then told a story about it, she realized, and so maybe the third doctor had come closest to the truth. Rather, she imagined the rat eating out of the wall, and as soon as she imagined it, she saw it, and then she told about it. But she couldn't honestly say she had made it up because the thought had come from nowhere, certainly not with her intention. What actually happened and what she made up became hopelessly confused for Ashanda, and there was something about this confusion she liked very much: She began to define herself by it.

It helped her write her stories. And (though I know it is considered bad form for a mother to talk this way to a son, even a grown son) it helped her in sex. Neither stories nor sex could ever be dull, of course, because there was always some unexpected layer of things in the stories and some unexpected innovation in the sex (a stranger, suddenly, in bed with her; an audience watching; the bed transformed into a moon) that turned every experience from the mediocre into the unusual.

Meanwhile, Daniel, as you have often reminded me from the adventurous cliff of your twentieth year, I lead a rather dull life, and when Ashanda screamed or wrote or made all sorts of trouble for the neighbors, I was as embarrassed and ashamed as anyone. All the while, however, in a secret world where shame was unknown and guilt was alleviated magically with words, she reigned supreme, magnetic, self-righteous, truly powerful, yet chronically out of control.

The house, after the babies came, was never properly cleaned. I compromised with minimal needs for order—vacuuming once a week, washing dirty dishes every night. But Venetian blinds, for instance, defeated me long before I might have picked up a rag to wipe their streaked, plastic slats of grime. I settled for leaving them opened so that only the slick edge was visible. It never occurred to me to take them down, that perhaps Venetian blinds were in and of themselves a ridiculous tyranny to a mother of small children or indeed to any person whose attention was not focused on domestic ordering. The point is, I failed to notice the pragmatic solution because each time I looked at those filthy blinds, I felt an edge of self-defining satisfaction.

In argument it was the same. At a certain point in a debate, I lost my temper. I could feel the loss like a tangible funnel of wind, or a high-tide wave in my throat, move into my mouth, and I would begin to shout. Words came easily, sentences constructed themselves perfectly in some mysterious process in my brain. Arguments lined up waiting to be made, extra ammunition the complete stock of which was never required. "Out of control," my enemies would mutter. But admirers praised me for conviction, marveled at my articulation, laughed good-humoredly at my willingness to enter into verbal battle with anyone under the sun. It was a verbal quality that some people associated with sexual passion, and when I was in my stride, shouting, I did feel sexual—visible, uninhibited, aroused. I would be making love with Bruce while another part of me was off to the side, directing, constructing the right movements, watching him as he watched me watching him. Mirrors of desire. Layers of conviction that clearly—though not clear to me at the time—rose dangerously out of the swamps of doubt. Daniel, as any psychologist will by now have predicted, beat me at my own game eventually, at least in verbal jousts (I don't know about his sex). In more ways than one I give him credit for changing me for the better, though I know he has paid a substantial price.

There were many times during his childhood when I raged at him. I berated him loudly, all the while wanting to stop, hating myself, not knowing where to turn to find a hand that might cover my mouth. Bruce did not interfere—not until much later in the evening when he might say, "Don't you think you were a little hard on him?" And the understatement would ignite my anger again.

Daniel developed a clarity about these rages that soothed me, and a detachment from me that, when he first described it, frightened me to the core. He could not have been more than eight years old when, following one of our battles, I asked him to tell me what he felt like when I yelled at him that way. "You don't deserve it," I told him. "It's really me who's at fault." We were sitting on the corner of his bed, clutching each other tightly, as if we were siblings, common victims of some third person, an abusive mother.

"I feel like I'm sitting far away in my brain, and I can see that I'm not the bad person you are yelling at," he said. Then we joined together in our condemnations of the woman who made him feel that way.

The moment I was out of his presence and thus my need to protect him, I joined with her again and for weeks suffered the worst and most uncontrollable shame I have ever known. My lack of control, during those rages, was no lie. I did not know who was speaking through my mouth, but it didn't feel like myself. I was, I thought then, taken over by some other voice, and there was no visible Julia to shut the mouth of the Julia who was doing the screaming. Now, years later, when we have talked about it dozens of times, when he has insisted on his forgiveness, when I have proven my faithfulness and my resolve, when he has even demonstrated strengths of character related to that early capacity to distance himself from unjust and inexplicable pain, I still remember him cowering at the edge of the bed as I shouted and accused, and the memory is worse in a way than the experience because now I know the name of that "stranger" who took over my mouth, the girl who believed in the omnipotence of feeling and the dark magic of words.

I am sitting in a small library on a street I walked a thousand times as a girl. What has become a library was once a courthouse attached to a women's prison. But the prison has been torn down and the ground where it stood transformed into a carefully planted community garden. As soon as I enter the reading room, I feel a wave of happiness, a sense of possibility like a shaft of light. Soft noise surrounds me, the shuffling of librarians' feet, books being pulled from the shelves, muted whispers and coughs. Then suddenly it will cease for a moment, and there is a split second of silence, like the silence at high tide when the waves pull back and seem to wait an instant before they slap the shore again. I can hear pages being turned. I feel a peace that comes from being away from home, from you, and all the associations of obligation, competing desires, loss, failure, hope. Sitting in the library in my old neighborhood, this notebook opened to begin, I knew I would not write about my childhood because for the first time in my life I felt done with it. It will come back to haunt me again, I suppose, but now, in my forties, I look back on it as something past, no longer compelling me to words. Two years ago, my sister and I visited our mother's grave on which I had long ago scattered our father's ashes. We found the grave untended. I had never paid the cemetery's bill for Perpetual Care. The long grasses and overlapping vines, even the sharp brambles, pleased us. My sister is a painter, and she took a rubbing of the gravestone by spreading white paper across it and brushing it with soft charcoal. She planned to use the rubbing either in a piece or as an amulet to enable her to draw the portraits of our parents that would change her image of herself. When she was done, I used her charcoal to add our children's names—your names—to the genealogy on the stone: Wife of _____; Mother of _____. Now, at least until the next rains, she would be a grandmother too. We cried, and then we left.

Now I teach in this neighborhood. I have walked down my old block so often it no longer pierces my consciousness with the jolt of memory, dislodging the present. I walk calmly, even distractedly, past my old home, and if I am with a friend, I may point casually to the second-floor windows and say, See? That is the room where my parents died. And that high-riser across the street replaced six brownstones, each painted a different shade of yellow or blue.

How much easier it would be to think of my childhood instead of always thinking of you. How comforting, all these years away from his death, to recall my father's habitual tyrannies, the many ways in which his chronic depressions caused him to neglect me. (He lies on the couch, interminably reading, his deaf ear turned toward the world, to my voice, until I say I am going out, and then he hears me and, full of self-pity and true loneliness, he looks at the ceiling, slowly lowers his eyelids, sighs once, deeply, until he knows I will remain at home.) How nostalgic to go even farther back in time, to his powerful years, the time when his conviction about all things mag-netized me so completely that even today its shadow in a man can thunder over language until my thoughts them-selves have been obliterated by sexual desire. What a re-lief it was to write of my mother's early death when it seemed primarily an abandonment of me. How easy to write of one's childhood, the time when I was acted upon, the hero in the story of the development of the self.

It would be easy to write in the voice of the daughter, finding causes in early deprivations to explain later faults. It is the mother's voice that cracks gratingly with shame and chronic self-doubt.

When Anthony was twelve years old, he was seriously depressed for several months. You, Daniel, used to com-plain about his hypochondria, his dependency, wanting him to be more like your father, like you. "Tell me, An-thony," I actually begged him once. "What is bothering you?" I had anxieties about drugs, visions of suicidal pro-portions. You shouted angrily, "It's just hard to get used to a new school, Mom. Will you stop exaggerating every-thing?" Still, I sat on his bed, stroking his hair, and for the first time in his life I felt him pull away from my em-brace. "I don't want to tell you," he said in a tone of someone who has been betrayed. "But why? Whatever it is I will understand." "Of course you will," he said with an edge of contempt. "And there isn't anything that spe-cial wrong." (It was only the adjustment to a new school, as you said, the terrible time of being a stranger, an out-sider to a group of children who had been together since they were toddlers.) "It just doesn't matter if I tell you what it is," he told me, jerking his forehead away from my hand. "The point is there is nothing you can do."

But Anthony, I wanted to cry out, we have to give you the illusion of safety, of order, or so we are told. We tell you that you must go to sleep because "that is what chil-dren do at eight o'clock," and we read you ancient poems on the subject from old, dog-eared books. We learn to order your meals, to add new foods at the right time, to cut food into bite-size pieces too small to stick in a child's throat. We wash and fold and pile clean shirts, sweaters, learn to patch corduroys, lengthen jeans; then a month or two later we prune closets and drawers of outgrown clothing, piling it into boxes for some other mother's smaller child. Our lullabies are filled with assurances that nothing can harm you, at least not until you spread your wings and take to the sky. We are instructed, and it does seem right, to place all sorts of boundaries around chaos for you—rules, orderly rooms, assurances that, no, we will not die until you are grown, only to sit silently by your bed, a decade hence, while you tell us accurately that there is nothing we can do.

And all that folding and ordering was easy compared to trying to keep up with the stages of your life when, as your body seemed to change before my eyes (you once said you could not judge the distance from the door to your shoulder, your arm was growing so fast, so you often missed the keyhole, bumping your fingers into the knob), truth too seemed to change daily, each blissfully known thing becoming unknown before I could catch my breath. Just as in the end of each story, or novel, I feel the joyful relief of formal completion, resolution of some sort, replaced almost instantaneously by the gnawing suspicion that it is a lie—those two hundred pages or so wrapped in a cover suggesting stories have final endings. And easy, too, those domestic contradictions and paradoxes of fiction compared with this journal in which I am forced to confront the limits of my control over the boundaries of my own story. I am trying to write my way out of silence, and the price seems to be remembering the very story I didn't want to tell.

For years, the battles with Daniel continue. I hate his iron-willed determination to decide everything for himself. He hates my too strict rules, my oversensitivity to noise, my iron will, a match for his. Neighbors suck in their breath when I appear in the hallway after a bad fight. And however sweet our reconciliations, however complete our forgiveness of each other, I can never forgive myself. It is not my point of view I question, but my intensity, the very quality that had once filled me with defiance and fierce pride. The intensity pushes me over an edge of self-control. It is my shouting, my head-splitting rage, my monstrous voice that causes me shame. After one fight, starting with a typically mundane conflict over whether or not to rinse dishes before stacking them into the dishwasher, screams escalate until Bruce and Anthony are rushing for other rooms. We are no longer interested in dishes, of course. I am accusing him of being unreliable, arrogant, impossible to live with, insensitive to other people's needs. He is defending himself against my wild escalations. As he insists that the dishes are no longer the issue and he certainly will not do or discuss them. I feel myself sinking into ever-deeper panic, as though *only* if he does the dishes will the world stop spinning out of control. Finally, Daniel punches the table and stalks off, slamming his bedroom door. A moment later Anthony slips out and joins Bruce in his room. A half hour passes while I clean the kitchen furiously, scouring the oven, mopping the floor, washing months of grime off the shelves. Then I am done and sitting at the table, I begin to consider the validity of Daniel's argument.

"You want to control everything, everyone," he had shouted, pointing a finger. "No, let me finish, let me fucking finish. You can't have everything exactly the way you want it to be." Beneath the anger, our similarities bind us together in mutual confusion. But, "No. I am not confused," he would assure me. "You may be confused, but I'm not. I see it all as clear as day. You want to control the world."

I am in a large house, a mansion, walking through many rooms. Some rooms are elegant and well cared for. The living room, for instance, is palatial. Large wooden beams stripe the ceiling which is two stories high. Here and there, turquoise pillows break the blinding white of the furniture. The large country kitchen containing a refrigerator that makes ice, a dishwasher, a corner pantry stocked with enough food and supplies for weeks, and a large table, also has plenty of room for three kinds of ovens—an ordinary oven, a microwave, and an old coal stove just for show. A long table that can seat twelve dominates the dining room. A patio faces the pool. . . .

But between the kitchen and dining room is another, smaller kitchen. From its broken wall old, stained porcelain shelves tip oddly, laden with dusty tools. Ugly knick-knacks of fat elves and broken ducks pile up in a grimy corner. Here, the ceiling bulges precariously through broken beams.

Upstairs, it's the same story. A master bedroom: large, color-coordinated, carpeted. A child's room wallpapered in pink roses, another in *Star Wars* decor—girl and boy neatly welcomed to the aesthetics of their respective worlds. There is a bathroom equipped with all modern conveniences for the maintenance of cleanliness—a glassed-in shower stall with a detachable nozzle that not only washes but massages as well.

And yet, just behind the *Star Wars* room is a series of smaller rooms that constitute an apartment within the house (for the maid? an aging grandmother invited to visit with tenuous welcome?). In this bedroom fabrics are mixed haphazardly, stripes and plaids, electric orange and faded green. The rug is threadbare. An ancient black-and-white television offers a pattern of snow to a background of persistent static. Adjoining this grubby room is a cramped bathroom in which a narrow shower stall is stained with yellow patterns behind a cotton curtain threaded with rivers of mildew. A medicine cabinet rattles off its hinges on the plaster-cracked wall.

I am not in a dream—though I have often had this dream

of old, neglected rooms suddenly discovered behind the wall or through the closet of my ordinary, orderly home. In the dreams, I know I cannot manage or control these new rooms, corners teeming with dust and life, though I try valiantly to peel off yellowed wallpaper, apply fresh paint, haul corroded furniture out the door. Walking through my friend's summer house, I remember my old dream, and I know that for some time I have been living desperately in the front rooms, resisting even a glance at the musty back ones, fearing they will always be there and at the same time fearing I have lost them for good.

In the front rooms, I practice competence, the sort of control that offends no one. I order and clean, design and fold, place furniture here, to please the eye and encourage conversation, arrange bookshelves by topic one year, by alphabet the next. These rooms send me into the world of jobs, maternal obligations, domestic tasks. From their orderly interiors I go forth to parent-teacher meetings, the dentist, the succession of gynecologists who ponder, scientifically, why when I am too young to be menopausal, my periods have all but stopped.

In the front rooms I tried for years to master ordinary competence, a maternal capacity that reportedly comes intuitively to most. But the back rooms are always just down the hall, through a door that will not close properly, tempting and frightening. Daniel, in his refusal to obey front-room instructions, backs me into those other places where panic replaces reason and the only way to control anything is to control the entire world.

From behind the closed door of Daniel's room comes the music of his saxophone. Slowly, with very few mistakes, he is picking out the melody of "Summertime," his favorite lullaby of all the songs I sang to him at night. I listen to the halting tones and recall the old lyrics—*nothing can harm you, with Mama and Daddy standing by*. Soon, he has mastered whole phrases, a complete verse, and he begins again, the four lines of music played over and over until the tone is clear, the long notes sustained above a husky undertone, all his heart and soul in that music, his forgiveness and accusation merged into one enveloping, penetrating sound.

Finally, after years of explanations and failed resolutions, I swear to silence, to an end, if not to my anger then to my expression of it. At the slightest sign of conflict, I lean hard into a wall, push my back against the plaster for support, the hardness against my spine reminding me of my resolve. My throat literally constricts. My stomach jolts and becomes a knot of sharp pain. But I am watching, watching and thinking—what can this rage be? His powerful will, of course. His need to question everything. The ordinary, draining burdens of my ruthless image of instructive maternity. But beneath all that— something else, surely. Some stream of feeling that joins and makes turbulent beyond reason this other, more ordinary thing. I have no answer. A mother's early death. A father's tyranny, magnetism, depression. A daughter's construction of a story in which the only protection against fragmentation is the creation of a seamless whole. A world in which even ordinary control in a woman is received with contemptuous wariness. A time when strong mothers resurrecting a point of view entombed for centuries intimidate fathers and enrage sons. No single answer will ever come, not once and for all in some transcendent conversion. But I watch, standing against the wall, or locking myself in my room where I kneel on the floor, my fist in my mouth or the pillow in my mouth, until the worst passes.

I do not think of Daniel during these moments, his welfare, his rights, his faults, my love for him. At such times I feel no love for anyone. I am trying to turn a failed psychological battle into a moral one, trying to fool my mind into an old-fashioned engagement in which there is still the possibility of clean victory. I am forcing myself to this effort not because of love, but because it is right. Yet, only love for Daniel or Anthony could stimulate and sustain the effort. Nothing else in the world. Kneeling on the floor, backing into the wall, I think only of the moment before I go to sleep when the house will be quiet at last, perhaps a minute before midnight, and I will enter a note into my journal: the date. And then a number. Five days without screaming. Six.

In the months that follow I will break my resolve at times. But slowly I will learn how to remain silent in the face of powerful emotion, to trust the silence more than the emotion. I may never have complete control over my anger, but I do have control over my voice. And then I realize, or remember, that I have always had an ambivalent relation to silence—thwarting it at every turn, killing it with words, and seeking it too, in my husband's temperament and in the ironic solitude required to construct a confession to the world.

One night, I dream again the now recurring dream of the silence of the snow. I am lost in a strange neighborhood, in a blizzard. I hear the special silence of the city in the midst of a snowstorm at night—the cars stopped, the streets empty, the silence almost audible. And I slip into it. No longer frightened, as I was in earlier versions of the dream, I step into a dark and comforting place, the frozen heart of the blizzard. I hear the silence in my ears, feel it in my flesh. I am still, quiet, released beyond imagination. I lower my head to my chest. The muscles in my neck loosen.

Eight days. Nine.

I become infatuated with the idea of disguise, its possibilities. I look up the word in my thesaurus: "To appear unrecognizable, to hide or obscure one's real nature, as in: She disguised her hatred. A cover, a shield, a shelter, a veil. To cover one's tracks, hide one's trail, bury one's talent in a napkin." The female imagery surprises and comforts me: "Keep a deep, dark secret. Hold one's tongue." When the thesaurus slips into its usual paradoxical opposites, I dutifully make a note of them in my journal (*unrevealed, unexplored, unexplained, unsolved, untold, unknown, nobody the wiser*); but I purposely slide over their implications for now.

I notice that in order to accomplish the goal I have set for myself, I must be silent about many things, not only anger. I give shorter and shorter descriptions to my family of my comings and goings, tell fewer and fewer secrets to my friends. For the first time in my life as a teacher, I lose language in class. I stop midlecture, my thoughts sucked into obliteration by that blizzard-white silence, wondering what on earth I wanted to say. When I do talk or write I have a sense of listening to a stranger. I hear my own voice as if it is coming from a strange mouth. When this happens I fall into silence or tear up the page, confused, even scared, but no less determined.

At night, the only time I am not busy with work and chores, I roll my tongue around my mouth and feel its smoothness. I force myself to tolerate the irritating tickle on my upper palate, which I caress in small swipes, over and over, so I know it is there. At night, the inside of my mouth becomes a world—untended over months of isolation, pristine. Weeds grow and tangle into complex shapes. If I open my lips, rich, sensuous vines hang over my chin. The gums, once clean and pink, are gray now, encrusted with protective layers of soil. The teeth, once white, are black, like old rocks covered with sharp, ancient snails.

When I no longer have to press my body into a wall or push a fist into my mouth, I have made a note of the fifty-fifth day. "Have you noticed?" I ask Daniel. "Yes," he tells me with wide and, I imagine, appreciative eyes, but he says no more. I am watching him now from a new distance and I am in pain, it turns out, not so much from his actions and misbehaviors as from the distance. I watch a tall young man turn a hunched back to me, but I see a small boy standing at the end of a train platform. I am returning home from a two-day journey to another city, and Daniel is running toward me. At two, he already runs gracefully, and dodging thighs and suitcases that move aside to let him through, he leaps into my arms. Then he is sitting at a small table. His first day at full-day kindergarten, a new school where he knows no one. I wait at the side with the other mothers, willing to spend the day if necessary, until he is ready to stay alone. A girl at the end of the table repeatedly looks back at her mother and whispers silently, *Don't go.* Daniel motions me toward him and says, "Leave now, Mommy. I'll be much better off when I'm alone." Mothers of dependent children smile enviously when I tell this story, but I know it is emblematic, and so I focus on it like a talisman as I wait for rage to subside. As comforting as it may be to love people as self-defined as Daniel and his father, it also leaves me feeling empty-handed, as if the only gift I could find is judged superfluous. Why was my anger at Anthony always containable? He could be as annoying as any other child, but his provocations never induced real rage. And when I think of the difference I am flooded with memories of Anthony's need for protection. Nightmares, stomach pains, until he was thirteen even social mishaps made him want shelter. When he was small we played a game in bed of making a tent from a blanket. Outside the tent lurked all kinds of danger, and our pleasure was the luxury of the safety inside. Shelter made Daniel feel as though he were sentenced to a cell. Or, from his earliest years the sort of shelter I offered was too untrustworthy to risk— shelter from my own worst self. Or, he would have been a boy like his father in any case. Or (for Anthony reacts now in similar ways), Daniel grew up inordinately fast. Or, there is not much difference between them except in my imagination, in the child's eye whose vision was formed and irreversibly distorted by an early, dumbstruck acquaintance with death, even the most neutral boundary feeling like a tombstone to me. I stare silently at my nearly grown son and take note of all sorts of difference. It is as if someone, everyone, has died and I am alone as I knew I was, I now remember, before Daniel was born.

In two months, I have neither raised my voice nor cried. But I have grown able to control my mouth in all sorts of situations—when I am in strong disagreement with someone, when someone is shouting unjustly at me, when I need something no one will provide. It's not simply a swallowing of words but, increasingly, a relief of anger I am feeling. I cannot say exactly what I am no longer angry about, but a burden has lifted. A sense of deprivation has always bound me to others in ready rage, but deprivation implies that someone has failed to provide. Now, I am aware instead of disappointment, an unbridgeable distance between myself and the world. I like this feeling of being a different sort of woman, someone with secrets, self-contained. Like some children, I feel protected by the rules of conduct I've constructed for myself.

But soon I am sick. Chronic, sharp pain I cannot alleviate races through my abdomen several times an hour. My doctor warns me that some unusual stress has caused an illness that I must quickly treat with medication before it becomes more serious. "Something has shocked your system," he says. I react to this diagnosis with pride. I have images of Arctic explorers withstanding terrible physical punishment in order to reach the pole, of triathlon racers losing control of their bowels as they stagger across the finish line. What are their sacrifices compared to my knotted stomach, my cracked and alien voice? Sitting on the examination table, my legs flung girlishly over the side, touched that someone has noticed the sign of the extremity of my effort, in the middle of the sixty-seventh day, I almost begin to cry.

~ Every summer, in a river near my friend Joanie's house, I swim to clear my head. The river begins near a narrow beach crowded with families from a surrounding town. But after a dozen yards or so it winds around a curve, and you are alone between tree-lined banks with no space for bathers to sit and sun themselves. Trees arch over the water. Every summer, for the weeks I live there, I watch Joanie, a more practiced and graceful swimmer than I, and I try to translate her movements into my own body when I begin my daily swim. Her stroke is balanced, her kick hardly visible, yet efficient, like a perfectly paced motor. She seems to move slowly, yet she makes tracks, passing other swimmers, then comes ashore tired and exhilarated after an unbroken mile. I dive in, slowly point my body upward, through the muddy layers of dark, cold water. But then the trick is to move as much as possible along the surface. Don't let the legs sink. Keep them straight with a swift, shallow kick. Arch the back, then round it slightly. Concentrate on your form and you will increase your pace. Keep yourself as much as possible on the surface until it seems, when you have hit your best stride, as if you are swimming over, not in, the water.

How tempted I am, now, to return to the surface. To describe some place, or incident, some character who is simultaneously me and not me. I would not write an experimental story (in which I intrude on "her" experiences, writing about myself in the third person), but a straightforward old-fashioned narrative where nothing breaks the unity of form. I would cut out of this confession (this bridge I am constructing to some other muddy bank I can't even see clearly) the material I have just set down about Daniel, the experience of losing my friend Martha, which still remains to be told. I would tear these pages from their binding, cut out the most identifiable details. (Change the color of my curtains, the names of my children, the memory of Daniel's face, afraid of me.) I would add humor, those easily written funny scenes all parents have stacked up in their minds like too many old letters stacked on a shelf, falling over: scenes of children and adolescents making their clumsy way to maturity, always testing the boundaries of fearful ignorance by exaggerating what they know. (Once, when he was fifteen, Daniel argued with me for an hour about what it felt like, in the 1950s, for a girl to wear her first bra. "Can't you give me the benefit of the doubt, of superior knowledge," I finally yelled at him, "in this if in no other area?" But he insisted on his right to imagine things for himself.)

Mercilessly, I would weed and prune the language of every single extraneous phrase, whole sentences of too explicit description, until the words in this notebook are as graceful and light as a stone skipping over water. I would render the inner life a place of rigorously undescribed mystery, no layers of consciousness pushing through, only the bare edge of what is visible put into language so that meaning can be elegantly encased in implication: a gesture, an action, a word, whole conversations and reflections of character hinted at in a double space. In nineteenth-century fiction the curtain dropped before even the suggestion of sex, birth, any bodily function. Now, we avoid the expression in language of meaning, counting on silence and precisely observed behavior to suggest what Charlotte Bronte took novels to explore.

It seems a small and innocent change to make up stories about "Julia," so harmless to allow myself the joyful epiphanies of writing fiction, the ecstasy of translation, the safety of the requirements of form. But for certain records, at certain times, formal balance, focus, the divisions of genre, even restrained language become masks themselves, distortions of these meaning-riddled decades of being a writer and a mother. (This is what the mother knew; this is what the writer felt; this is what the analytical thinker analytically thought.) I am looking for connections between experiences that are usually polarized, and I can begin to name these connections only if I allow the most formless layers of consciousness to break into the story.

I wanted to control the world with my words, to affect history with a sentence perfectly framed. If I wrote well enough, I thought, the world would see me, hear my meaning; my dead parents might hear me and know me perfectly at last. I wanted to control the world for my sons, protect them from cars turning corners too fast, from small-minded ignorance about the nature of manhood which seeps into their postures as their bodies become suddenly, obviously gendered. (Square jaws from soft, rounded chins. Hands twice the size of my own.) Loving something (writing) or someone (children) closely identified with the self requires separation to survive whole: I must exist apart from it so that the inevitable losses, rejections, failures, will not kill me. But I resist: the distance robs me of ecstasy even as it frees me from imprisonment in the infantile connection—the belief that I can be perfectly revealed, perfectly known.

Both mothering and writing require that passion be contained, domesticated by physical care or craft. At times, hugging a small child, I have felt the desire to take

him back inside, hug him to death, bind him to me, refusing any outside risk to his being and therefore my own.
Revising language of a story that has been written in a
moment of inspiration can seem to be an imposition of
technical dressing on naked authenticity. Both resistances
are bound in paradox. The softer, more restrained embrace will strengthen the child. In repeated, careful revi-
sions of language, consciousness is deepened as the more
precise words clarify beyond the original inspiration. Yet
the child cannot be protected from knowing about the
fiercer maternal passions. And the beautiful formalities and
structures of prose can be used to hide the more disorganized truths of experience.

Both writing and mothering risk the possibility of failure as painful as any I know. Each in the beginning seemed
pristine, the work carrying within its initial sentences the
promise of brilliance, the children's unscarred flesh and
minds suggesting a crueler illusion—the perfect reparation
of myself. Instead, on each anvil, the finished book, the
child's mind, I have worked the reenactment of every lim-
itation by which I have always been encumbered. Looking back, books and years later, I see my worst faults and
have to fight against my temperamental pessimism to
notice the limited achievements, also real.

Two stories converge in my life, one about motherhood, the other about writing, and the result of the convergence is a silence so new and unambiguous, I cannot
escape its restrictions: say this, but not that; write this,
but not that. Both stories are about power—power
abused, denied, translated into the wrong words. The ac-
curate perception of one's own power (to create, to save,
to hurt, to tell, to withhold from telling) is the essence, I
think, of self-respect, but also of humility. Not to blame
oneself too grandly, but not to forgive oneself too easily
while imagining one's own actions are too insignificant to
cause real pain. A denial of power is potentially exactly
the same, in effect, as a claim to omnipotence. How easy

it would be, Daniel, to write in the daughter's voice, that voice that doesn't have to take the blame.

("There are some things which have to be said before you can press on to others." And, "One must eventually break the silence about difficult things." Both, Christa Wolf.)

How does a woman who does not write become a woman who writes again? The threads are entangled, but if I focus too carefully on form and reformulations, I will lose some of the layers as surely as the swimmer, concentrating on the most efficient, graceful movement of her arms, synchronizing with a swift but shallow kick, loses her consciousness of the depths beneath her and may suddenly find her arms and feet are bumping stupidly on the ground.

("[She] simply cannot manage to make her experience into a presentable story, cannot produce it out of herself as an artistic product. She cannot kill the experience of the woman she is in 'art.' " Christa Wolf.)

A woman who writes / a woman who does not write.

A lifelong need for silence. Certainly that.

A fear of exposure. No, that is what it was at first. Then it became an unwillingness to expose. Why, Martha said to me, are you willing to hurt me? It was a brilliantly constructed sentence. She might have said, for instance, Why are you going to hurt me? That was a question I could have answered. I am going to hurt you, I might have said, because that is the only way I can be myself. Or, she might have said, How can you hurt me this way? And I would have said, I am not doing it on purpose. Or, best of all, she might have said, Why must you hurt me this way? And I would have said, I don't know. But she knew what she was after, while I was silenced by the brilliant construction of her sentence.

Her hair was dark brown and hung to her shoulders in thick, kinky curls. Her skin was a sallow tan. Her eyes were black and sad, no matter the expression on the rest of her face, and this characteristic was both disconcerting and attractive to me. Her mouth was wide and, I admit, reminded me of my mother. She retained a clumsy posture from a grotesque case of adolescent insecurity, she said, but she was strong, and she could carry her five-year-old on her back long before I developed the strength to do so. We were alike in background and interests, both of us daughters of secular Jews who infused in us from earliest childhood a sense of obligation to the world. We read fiction and psychoanalysis as people like us might have read philosophy in the past, looking for moral clarity and direction. We had given birth to our children within the same five-year period and had both limited our work to part-time—mine as a writer and teacher, hers as a therapist—to take care of babies at home. But somehow, despite background and culture, Martha had become an athlete and achieved a notable competence in the world. I learned to cook huge meals from her, and to hike up mountains, though never to drive while she drove anything on wheels.

During the first years of motherhood, we met daily in the playground, balancing between the luxurious and deadening fatigue brought on by the relentless, routinized demands of caring for small children. At six P.M. on warm days when our suited, professional husbands came to the playground from work, arms spread to catch leaping children, we saved ourselves the full discomfort of a life so contradictory to our image of ourselves as outsiders and rebels by smirks and self-mockeries that split the real self (cynical social critics) from the ordinary middle-class mothers, trapped within the playground bars. Later, the two families would join for a large dinner, and we'd drink enough wine to get high. Then, to the consternation of our more conventional but also less hypocritical husbands, we'd mock our lives some more. On the other hand, there were real difficulties to manage. New and ignorant mothers, yet adhering to a merciless standard of perfection, we joined forces in a demanding education. On the phone each night, during rare quiet moments in the playground if the children napped, dirty and weary in their strollers, and at weekly dinners out we reserved for ourselves, we were philosophers of family relations, analyzing the distinctions between punishment and discipline, mapping the line between obligation to another and the rightful needs of the self. We complained of our husbands, but we were too strict moralists for contentment with that simple pleasure. So we blamed ourselves too, and gave careful credence to the historical changes that had demanded of Bruce and Eliot a far more attentive fatherhood than they had ever anticipated as boys. Still, I wonder now if our mutual complaints about them—their shared male failings as well as their particular faults, did not also strengthen our friendship and lead inevitably to that night when one sort of love seemed to extend very naturally into another. Martha thought so. That was as much a reason as my telling the story for her decision to end our friendship for good.

During the winter months, Martha's family used their country house only occasionally, especially when the children were babies and it was such trouble to move around with portocribs, carriages, dozens of changes of clothes. Eventually, though, Martha began going for weekends alone, leaving her children in the care of their father while she sought the only combination she knew for peace of mind: solitude, mountains, woods. Long before that weekend when she surprised me by inviting me to come along, there had been suggestions that our feeling for each other went beyond simple friendship. A gaze that momentarily included the energizing discomfort of sexuality. A desire to be in each other's presence daily. And, several times from Martha, whispered erotic remarks. "Your breasts are beautiful," she once murmured as we hugged. But when I looked at her, startled and excited, her face was ordinary, even blank.

I recall the feeling of being in some world where none of the ordinary rules applied. I thought about Bruce and Eliot, about the children, and it seemed to me they could not mind, at the same time as I believed they would never know. Martha and I lay in each other's arms listening to the wind, and it seemed as if when the wind stopped the night would exist apart from ordinary life, like an old-fashioned story with a real ending. I was covered warmly by Martha's taut body, her strong thighs against mine, then by the old patchwork quilt I had helped her find in a country store, and I felt a part of the wind. When I think back on that night now, I imagine the sky fading into a white glow of snow on the mountain, the dark outlines of trees, the shaking of panes in the red window frames. I see the darkened living room where the children's toys were piled in an old wicker basket and the dying coals in the black stove Eliot had built in. Then I see the stairs, a bit rickety and cold to the feet, and the small entranceway to the second story, the ceiling so low even I had to bend my head. The children's room. The guest room Bruce and I used. And then I see Martha's mouth and her sad, black eyes and I am touching her thick hair. I also hear her whisper, "We can never tell," in my ear. And, far more coldly, a voice without any tone of regret, in the car the next morning: "This can never happen again." I agreed, never dreaming that telling and writing a story would be, of course, the same thing to her.

For months afterward, only patterns of silence and resonant lies. We still meet for dinners occasionally, but at family gatherings Martha flirts with Eliot as though they are new lovers. She is warm to me, as a good hostess is warm to a little known guest. During my family squabbles, she develops a new identification with Bruce's point of view. Once, we even try a weekend at their country house, and when we arrive it is clear they have been robbed. Martha, who by now is much like a stranger to me, is devastated by what she calls the rape of her beautiful house. The stereo unit and an old Oriental rug are gone. Two windows are broken, and a veil of broken glass covers the hard wood floor. Outside, a single rose she has planted in a clay pot has been knocked over, the pot shattered, the rose dead. Immediately Martha begins to sweep, gathering glass and mud tracked in by the thieves. She sweeps more and more swiftly, and while she sweeps into corners, around moldings, she cries. As I watch her cry, I remember exactly why I have loved her. Beneath her self-containment and her competence, she is full of unmasked need, and she is innocent of either shame or denial when this need is ascendant. I was the only person, apart from Eliot, she could lean on, she could not do without, she often said. And I had been happily hooked for years on the sense of worthiness her need bestowed upon me. I want to embrace her, smooth her dark hair away from her heavily perspiring forehead, but by now I don't dare. Eliot and Bruce are straightening furniture, putting tables right, but when Eliot notices her tears, he drops everything and encloses her in his arms.

All that weekend I try to talk to her, but she insists she just wants to forget it: "Let's talk about something pleasant." She smiles and invites me into the kitchen to help her ready ingredients for one of Eliot's famous pumpkin pies.

I did not run home from that miserable ride in the car the morning after our night together and coldly design a story. Neither pain, nor guilt, nor love give rise to stories in me, but something between loss and desire, a need for consolation I can find only in words. It was that weekend, the image of her madly sweeping glass into a shimmering mountain in the middle of the floor, that left me with nothing to do but write.

I read my story to no one. Away from my enforced

charade with Martha, I tried, by reordering time and paying more careful attention to image and detail than I'd ever done before in my writing life, to comprehend what had led me to that night in her bed. I became so preoccupied and excited with what I was learning about structure and language—my expanding sense of control—the story itself seemed almost incidental. The fact that I was also exonerating myself of simple culpability and assuaging my guilt in relation to all of them did not often permeate, while I worked, the grace of the leap forward in craft. I was obsessed with my project, and that obsession enabled me to relinquish my obsession with permeating Martha's reserve.

She became increasingly distant from me, and during the six months it took me to write and sell my series of stories about what I lost and still wanted/what I no longer wanted and hadn't quite lost, and well before the time when I would see that our friendship might have ended anyway, Martha found Max. I submitted to her need to maintain something of our friendship, but according to Max's new rules. She'd be happy to listen to anything I had to say, she told me, but I shouldn't expect any confessions from her. Not that she was trying to distance her life from mine. It was simply that having found Max, she no longer needed me. "Max doesn't think I should discuss my problems with anyone but him. It interrupts the continuity of my therapy," she'd repeat with infinite patience when I asked how things were with her and Eliot. And if I persisted with questions, either innocent or provocative, she'd say, "It only feeds my masochism to complain." I can see very clearly, even now that years have passed, how her mouth tightened, and she seemed to square her shoulders as she faced me, staring at me with those sad, anachronistic eyes.

Aside from the publisher, I had told only Bruce about the stories, reading them aloud to him as I often did with my work. He had been the first person to encourage my writing, years before, insisting that the strength of my stories was my determination to discover what was true. Granted, he'd admit when pressed, it was the same quality that generated my worst faults: a merciless insistence on pursuing something despite another's need—his, for example—for withdrawal; my rages at Daniel. Still, I allowed myself to believe (because I needed his permission? because I wanted to hurt him into needing me?) that he might receive even this story as proof of talent rather than betrayal.

He was silent when I was done. "They're good," he finally said. And then, "Did it really happen that way?"

"Yes," I said. He stiffened slightly, handed me the pages, and put on his reading glasses, turning to his book. "It only happened once," I said, "and it won't happen again." He nodded without expression and remained stiff in my presence, in every situation, for weeks.

One night, I noticed his shoulders relax somewhat. It was late, and the children were long asleep. "Can you forgive me?" I asked.

"I already have," he said, and I knew exactly the nature of the loss Martha's distance had left me to endure. It was clear that I could no longer postpone telling her, too.

Bracing myself for her impenetrable exterior, which she had certainly possessed before "the break in the continuity of her personality" (she called it) represented it by her friendship with me, I met her for a walk. The streets were piled high with snow hills from a storm the day before, and the winter sun was slowly melting them into icy rivers, interrupting the smooth run of joggers who had to leap over and sidetrack them as they ran.

"How's his Maxness?" I asked.

"It's not funny or witty, Julia. I don't like it at all," she said, and I noticed for the third time a dramatic change in her voice I could no longer ignore.

"Your voice is funny. You're pronouncing things differently," I said. She flushed slightly as if I had told her she was beautiful.

"Why are you talking like that?" I insisted as we stepped around the soft mounds of melted snow.

"Like what?" She giggled.

"You know. Dentalizing your T's like that when you say *don'ttt*. You sound like your cousin Shirley from Queens."

She shrugged and looked down at the snow.

"And you're saying *loik* instead of *like*. What happened to that nonregional voice you've been working at all these years?"

"It must be Max," Martha answered. "I'm internalizing him."

I had been hearing this phrase—"internalizing him"—along with the word *grandiosity* from her for several months, while I noticed also a change in the structure of our conversations. I would tell her a long story about something worrying me, disobeying her new rules while hoping she would fall back into old conversations, but instead of offering the mirror of her own life, as she had promised she would not, Martha would say, "It's just your masochism, Julia." Or, "It's just your grandiosi*tsy*."

"Why are you diagnosing me?" I'd ask, critical in a new way.

"It's Max," Martha explained. "He's forcing me to accept myself. Look, when you're a child you internalize the object who cares for you. I had a bad mother who intruded on me endlessly. You know what she's like. But I internalized her anyway, took her voice in. We all do that. And when we behave in ways we don't want to—like when you yell at Daniel too much—it's not really us. It's your father talking, for instance. An internalization. Now I'm extricating that false self through my analysis. I'm internalizing Max."

"But there must be something wrong if you're begin-

138

ning to talk like him. You don't sound like yourself," I said.

"I'm not even sure you've ever known my true self," she answered fiercely. "I've always changed myself—trying to please you."

We walked deeper into the park until children on sleds disappeared and only a few lovers walked through the snow-covered lanes, stopping to kiss under branches outlined in ice. The snow drifts were so high that walking became difficult, and we turned back toward the avenue again. But we had gone farther than we'd realized, and it took almost an hour to reach the edge of the park. All this time, I talked, pausing for reactions from Martha that never came. Her silence caused me to become very anxious, which in turn caused me to increase the pace of my talking, as if the sound of my own voice could blot out her clear message that she didn't want to hear. I described a recent fight with Bruce, reminded Martha of fights she'd had with Eliot that were similar to mine. I tried to hold up both parts of the conversation. I emphasized the similarities in the fights, then swiftly, seamlessly, connected it all with more general historical forces. "This is a hard time for men and women, of course. It isn't Bruce's fault. It isn't Eliot's."

Martha said, "Julia, I work hard all week. I don't want to have these serious conversations on weekends. Can we please just enjoy ourselves? Look at the beautiful ice formations on those trees."

"It's easier for women loving women these days," I said, purposely trying her patience, not liking her real self as much as the one she'd made up for me.

She was quiet for so long I was afraid she might simply walk away, but soon she began to talk of simpler things which seemed to rouse her spirits. We walked along the avenue again, looked into a new shoe store where she tried on several pairs of pointed-toe, high-heeled pumps. "You like these?" she asked, lifting a long leg, pointing a slender foot for me to inspect the low cut, the narrow heel, the soft brown leather.

"They're beautiful. I wouldn't wear them, but they're beautiful on you," I said.

Martha responded as if she were reading lines from a dull script. "Why wouldn't you wear them."

"They're too uncomfortable. I hated them in the fifties, and I still hate them." I pulled my feet, clad in clumsy hiking boots, under the seat and caught a glimpse of myself in the mirror. My hair looked especially stringy, and I shoved it angrily behind my ears. Martha paid for the shoes and, smiling, her mood changed, said, "Come on, sweetie. Let's go."

Right before we parted, thinking, madly, that my action would save the past rather than confirm its ending, I gave her a copy of the stories, already printed in galleys, irreversibly bound.

Our final meeting, at her apartment, was truly our last. Bruce refused to come and tried to dissuade me from going. "She's got to be furious with you. She might even hurt you," he warned.

"Are you furious at me?" I asked, desperate for his anger since by now it was clear I would never have his forgiveness. He had been patient, tolerant, and cold for months. "I want no part of it," he said. But I went anyway, to hear—as she had said to me over the phone—what she thought of my stories. And, she insisted, Eliot would be there, too.

"Why are you willing to hurt me like this?" was the first thing she said, and I was silenced by the brilliant construction of her sentence.

Then she is shouting accusations at me, some painfully true, recalled from years of the most detailed knowledge of my dreams. Some are wide of the mark, but I do not interpret this bad aim accurately and am simply confused. I can see—there is no way to deny it—that she is clutching for control over me and the power I have stolen from her to reveal only what she wishes of her life. Yet I say something that is as perfectly constructed a sentence as her question to me, if my desire is to provoke her wildest rage, and all the while I think I am using the language of self-defense.

"You can't control what I do," I tell her haughtily, feeling helpless and full of doubt.

And she attacks me, leaping on me and throwing me back on the couch, kicking my shins with her heels while if I had not held her off an inch from my face, she would have bitten my cheek. Her powerful thighs pin me, but somehow I keep her mouth from my face long enough for Eliot, who up until then has remained silent, a passive witness to our battle, to begin shouting and pulling her off me.

When she is seated again, I remain. For a full hour I listen to her litany of accusations, her confessions of despair, her terror of exposure, her contempt for me and my writing. "Only mediocre writers use their own lives, their autobiographies," she sneers. "Real artists make things up." And since there is an echoing chorus waiting in the back of my mind for just this cue, my only response is silence. I cannot answer her questions, nor do I defend myself, yet when she asks if I will withdraw the stories from publication, I say no.

At last I leave, not because there is a break in the talking, nor because we have reached either partial resolution or certain impasse, but because at that moment it suddenly seems to me that I can get up and walk out, and I wonder why I have not done so before. I walk slowly down the street, trying to hold in the vomit that will erupt from me the moment I enter my apartment.

In the months to come, I will often lose time, finding myself lost on the streets. I will burn my arm in an oven, unintentionally. One dark night, I will fall down a steep cellar stair to the cement floor below, though my hostess

141

warned me, when she showed me the beautiful but unfinished bedroom in the light of day, that the unguarded stairway was there, to watch out for it in the middle of the night. I will run like a madwoman to my children's school to protect them from kidnapping snares, peeking in the glass window of the doors to their rooms to make sure they are safe. I will become another woman in bed with Bruce. First, I will crave his flesh only for comfort, a maternal embrace. Then, I will be unable to bear the touch of other flesh at all. Soon, I will return to the need for physical connection, but when we make love, which I still imagine myself to strongly desire, both desire and imagination will fail me until, somewhere near the ceiling, I look down on my monstrous self which is closed, unreadable and cold. In sex as in writing I am terrified of exposure, but it comes to me as a sense of incapacity, as if someone were asking me to speak Chinese, and I would comply theoretically, but I wouldn't know where to begin. And during all the years when clarity of any sort seems to be the greatest gift I can hope for in my life, I will always see with complete clarity her eyes. They were wide and full of sorrow. Sunk in a face as marked by rage as any I have ever seen, they still conveyed that terrible sadness, as isolated from everything else in the room as a solitary child screaming in the chaos and rubble of a bombed city in the middle of a war.

And I have no trouble recalling precisely the chill in her voice when she said, "You betrayed me." It was a familiar coldness she had assumed before with me, with everyone, even her children, and which had always angered me even as it magnetized my attraction and created the terms of my love. (She was wearing an antique man's shirt that day, light green, and the wide collar hung gracefully around her slender neck.) But she was betraying me, I thought then, by acting for Eliot's benefit as though I had been the canny seductress, she the naïve victim of one night's madness unconnected with the rest of our lives.

Now, I see she was right. I betrayed her with my stories first, and in order to incorporate that capacity for betrayal all my assumptions about art, obligation, and love came into question. Storytelling itself no longer seemed a noble thing, and my willingness to hurt Daniel with my screams assumed a devastating connection to the pain I caused Martha with my storytelling voice.

Privately, like an exile studying a map that might some-day get her home, I wrote out and framed for the wall near my desk that twisted turning point in the thesaurus's associations to disguise: unrevealed; unexplored, unexplained; unsolved; untold; unknown; nobody the wiser. But in my daily life, the scheduled, busy waking hours I had come to think of as most real, I valued silence and restraint. Whatever self-denial those new values brought was outweighed for years by a sense of pride and safety I achieved. And only now, when a woman who writes is locked inside the silence of a woman who does not write, do I begin to consider there are other questions to be asked, and I see the price I have paid for the suppression of a passion by which I always defined myself and whose release was found only in sex and words.

～ "I do not understand why you're not bleeding," the third in a carefully selected succession of gynecologists said to me in my forty-first year. "You are too young for menopause, and indeed the vaginal environment is not menopausal according to the test. Some trauma, perhaps?" she asked. "Some unusual anxiety precipitating the change of life?"

"Oh come on, Mom," you say to me in your *don't give me those perfectly apt metaphors* tone.

"No, really, Daniel. It's true. I stopped menstruating after those stories came out. And that's when I stopped having those rages at you."

"That was always exaggerated too," you say to me. "Why do you always exaggerate everything? You've always been a good mother. You screamed too much, that's all. I never think about it anymore." You stand up from the table and tower over me, suggesting superior knowledge I want more than anything to rely upon, your tone conveying the old conviction of Ashanda, that girl I have not heard in years. "The only thing I really hate about you is how much you repeat everything, and how you don't listen to me, and how you exaggerate everything," you say.

"That's three things, Daniel."

"As you've often said to me, don't be so literalistic."

"So I'm making it up? All these memories of my anger and how it must have hurt you?"

"You're not making it up. You're just exaggerating its importance." And you flip open a beer, take a long swig. "Not only that," you continue, just when I am hoping for a reprieve, "you remember things wrong. Like I say I'll be home between two A.M. and two-fifteen, and you remember that I said two, so when I get here you're sitting at the kitchen table smoking, instead of lying in your bed asleep, where you ought to be." You finish your beer and stare at me. Evening light breaks in through the parting of the green plaid curtains that cover the terrace door. The sound of the television can be heard from the bedroom where Bruce is watching the news, and I long to escape you and join him to be comforted by his habitual silence, which I have insisted I deplore. But you, with my mouth and my eyes, are midlecture, and I listen, magnetized, as you question the accuracy of my remembrance.

And the story of Martha? Pure fiction in the sense my students mean the word: I made it up. I merged three stories into one, calling them all "Martha" just because I thought I saw some identity in the three. I have told a lie in effect, a fiction passed off as autobiography rather than the other way around. But it seemed far too complicated to explain to Daniel that there was a kind of truth in the fiction of Martha. Also, it would have been unfair, because at eighteen he was understandably more comfortable with the lie at the heart of my autobiography than with my fiction as the heart of the truth.

I saw Martha on the street the other day, the first time in six years. Politely, I said hello. She asked me questions about my life—how were the children? how was I? Fine, I said, and how are you? Fine, she said. But when she looked directly into my eyes and said it was hard to think of her older daughter going away to college next year, I said, yes, it had been very hard when Daniel left and tears threatened. Then I felt ashamed and quickly returned to small talk so I could get away. But on my way home, I said in a low whisper, Yes, Martha, it is hard to watch your children grow up. And isn't it strange the way your work can seem less definitive in your forties than it did in your twenties and thirties, even though you do it with greater love? Isn't it painful and odd that you fear you could live without it, as you could never live without your children? I remember the first day you went back to work after the children were no longer babies, and you'd hired a sitter to care for them during the afternoon. You were carrying a brand new attaché case when I met you on the street and said, "Oh, Martha, you already have a briefcase full of work!" But you smiled your wonderful self-mocking smile and flipped it open for me to see its empty interior. (I think there was a pen and a small pad inside.) "I just want to carry it," you said. "It makes me feel real."

You were always so convinced by appearances; I mean that in a complimentary way. You taught me to value external life—a room well designed, a meal served beautifully, an especially elegant blouse—the form of a thing, and so my writing would not have been the same without you. When you asked me how I was, how the children were, I believe you were not dissembling. You wanted the outlines, at least, and I wanted your outlines too. Yet, telling you this as I walked home alone, I was satisfied, as I never would have been when you knew me, by the deeper silence between us. We talk to each other, I see now, from various levels of narration, and the central layer has no monopoly on truth. The fiction is not that many distinct narrators are manifestations of the writer's voice, but that the writer, or anyone else, can be defined by only one. We are at the heart of the stories we write, and we are wandering around the circumference, folding our children's clothes, editing our students' stories, too.

And now I am thinking of Mary Shelley, that teenage

mother, a motherless daughter of a powerful father, constructing her famous novel of a monstrous creature so recognizable and human that it instantly became myth. Of the circle of narrators, each one penetrating a little deeper into the truth. And how interesting, I tell my students with a gleam in my eye, that all these narrators are male, even the one at the center, the monster himself, telling his story of orphanhood, pitiful yearning for love, murderous rage at not being loved enough by anyone in return. Like any responsible teacher of literature, I have learned that the three narrators in that novel of birth giving and art—the distanced storyteller, the obsessive creator, the monster—are all one, all female, all Mary herself. Dutifully, I have followed the text, found the unmistakable allusions to motherhood, to an artist's guilt for exposure and ambition that can only be female, the belief that all hell will break loose, all loved ones destroyed, the self condemned to exile, if she persists in her monstrous creation—the story of her life. What astonishes me anew every semester is the blush of recognition on the faces of the young women when I first utter the phrase: the monstrous self. Coming of age in the late 1980s, postfeminist, postmodernist, poststructuralist, still at the heart of the matter is the huge, unloved, shameful intellectual female monster, bound to tell her story again and again, the writer both trapped and freed at the heart of her text.

Martha's ability to stick to the proper forms, graceful and eloquent, still entrances me, just as I sigh with admiration when the language of fiction soars above the dark water like a perfectly skipped stone. But I am not a stone, not even always a swimmer. I dive down. I want books to crash into my body and move me. I want the voices of real men and women weaving their lives into mine.

"Everything's fine," I said to you on the street while checking out the length and color of your hair (mine has gone gray, you see), the new lines at the corners of your eyes, your mouth. And from the central voice, now silent in your presence: It was not that I wanted to hurt you. But apparently I was willing to hurt you if it meant I could write my story for the world.

After three years of a sequence of doctors, one woman finally said to me from behind her wide marble desk: "You have entered menopause at an unusually early age. Whatever the process that curtailed your menstruation, it is now complete. The trauma is over." Through a window behind her desk I can see into a loft across the street. A bright lamp stands in the corner. An attractive pink couch is nestled against the wall. The walls around my doctor's desk are white with barely a tint of blue. On her right, a photograph of her daughter and herself—black and white, their hair blown by what must have been an ocean wind. The surface of her desk is empty except for a neat appointment book, a silver pen, a bran muffin on a white napkin. The colors and shapes are so blindingly clear, I have to close my eyes.

"And anyway," Daniel is saying to me, "I never understood why you write that way."

"What way?"

"All mixed up—things that really happened and things you made up."

"Because it seems the only way to get at the truth. To resist the well-made story, the fetish of art."

"But those stories . . ." He shakes his head, impatient and uncomprehending, yet trying to understand. "Those so-called Julia stories. It's not really fair, Mom. You make me say things I'd never say just to make a point. Like you made me into a symbol of distance in that one called 'Penetrations.' I'm the bad guy. Anyone can see that." He opens the refrigerator and grabs a quart of juice, raises the carton to his mouth.

"Can't you get a glass, Daniel? For God's sake. How many times do I have to tell you boys not to drink from the quart?"

"In almost every one of the stories," he answers, grinning.

Ignoring this victory, I respond to his previous accusation. "I'm trying to be honest, to write what seems true to me."

"Well, you have all the control," he says. "It isn't fair. You make me what you want me to be."

"No, it's you who make me what you want me to be," I respond. "You made me into a mother. I didn't know how to do it. Oh, feeding you and dressing you and taking care of you—that was pretty easy to learn. But I had to tell you what to do. You think I was always sure what I was saying was the truth? Or that I'm sure now? You make me into a mother every day."

"You always sound pretty sure," he tells me, taking long gulps from the carton of juice. Silently I hand him a glass, which he ignores, and giving me a look of exasperation he walks out of the room. I hear him take out his guitar. Before music begins to blast he shouts from his room, "Obviously *you* made *me* up. They're *your* stories. I'm *your* child."

Every December when they were small, we cuddled on a disheveled couch watching simple Christmas cartoons on television. When they were in bed, I sat by their sides humming songs my parents sang to me. In the summer when the ocean was at low tide, sometimes a safe, shallow channel of water would form between the beach and a sand bar, and along with other weary parents I sat dreamily in the mud watching them sift sand and try to trap water in plastic colanders. I remember feeling during those times, when there was no threat to their safety, even their endless words stopped by the dark bedroom, the hypnotic cartoon, the easy shallow waves and the mud, that I was contentedly myself. No mask, no disguise, nor any self-assertion struggled for in language was necessary for a moment. I was not a woman in the process of definition, of creation, but in some other placid state I had never

150

otherwise known. And so it must be that all the unsafety of my life caused me to write, first for my mother and now for my sons. I am constructing a tapestry of dark, thick, layered words to ward off dangers, and my accomplishment will never last much longer than the ephemeral relief of completing a final page.

Once I had a single voice, defined by conviction, laced with passion, thrusting its language into the world. Then I lived some years with none, or so it felt to me, because no matter how normally I spoke or occasionally wrote, the sounds echoed in my ears as if from some incorporeal spirit lost in the snow. Now it seems I have two, three, multiple voices, one making up stories, one trying to describe the literal truth, one—thoughtful and unspontaneous—searching for the right thing to say to a son.

I sit down at the table wishing I could drop the whole thing, the masks of motherhood, the burdens of art. The music of Daniel's electric guitar fills the house—a high melody, a heavy downbeat inside my head. I know so little about music, and he is so different from me. Against that realization my desire for silence and transformation took root. For who was I screaming at, whose badness trying to suppress, whose helplessness denying and confirming in one terrible shout? Certainly not Daniel's. The price of giving up magic has left me with a sense of normality that can sometimes feel like mediocrity and failure, and I am always mapping the distinction. But I know from my students that self-indulgence is not the telling and retelling of one's own story. It is a willingness to excuse one's own moral blindness, the infantilizing sanctuary of a lifetime bound by one point of view.

I am quiet in my chair. The lights in the house are dim, and there is a coolness in the air. Then wearily I rise, because otherwise I may remain in this spot forever, content and fatigued until I die. Carrying a glass in one hand, a fresh quart of juice in the other, stalking my son, I say,

"Daniel, I want to keep talking." And holding out the quart and the glass, I add, "Your choice." But he is engrossed in his music, some harmony of blues with contemporary jazz he makes up himself.

THREE

~

Worlds Beyond My Control

~

Yes: to be rid of your own soul, to be able to look your mother boldly in the eye as she sits on the edge of your bed in the evening, wanting to know if you have told her everything: But you must tell me everything. To lie brazenly: Everything, yes! When you know deep down: not everything, not ever again. Because that's impossible.
       —Patterns of Childhood,
        Christa Wolf

But you said there was no defense.
"There ain't."
Then what do I do?
"Know it, and go out the yard. Go on."
       —Beloved, *Toni Morrison*

～ I am forty-five years old. I have two sons, one is gone from home. The other's leaving gathers energy like a storm off the coast, and I have known hurricanes before. I begin the dreary process of battening down hatches, taping windows, packing breakables in layers of newspaper, then laying them in cartons. At night, when Anthony is out on the street, I lie in my bed and practice putting old habits away as if they were china plates I'd hoped to save forever. I cannot protect him, I tell myself in the dark. Even if at this very moment some mugger is poised for attack, even if he is lying damaged, cut and bruised, even if I imagine every possible danger and like a witch think it away, I cannot protect him. I have no control, I tell myself in the dark. There is nothing I can do now. His life. My life. Separate as sentences.

Yet once I knew, when he toddled into ponds unsteady on chubby legs, when he dared to swing too high, his exuberance always dominating caution, that if I maintained a constant vigilance I could negate the threat of injury. I held up my arms to slow speeding cars. I followed him at a distance the first day he walked alone to school. I ate his bottled peaches first, in case of botulism.

Freak accidents occur. Children die. A woman of thirty, I reached to clutch him from too deep waters in the pond warning, "Stay in the shallow, Anthony, or you can't go in!" There was conviction in my voice. It's not only their ages but my own that makes me prey to doubt.

Last week, for instance, Anthony was outrageously fresh to me in front of guests, and I swore I'd punish him as I'd punished them both for freshness since they were small. Proudly, I'd point to my achievement. In a tough, loud time, I'd made polite and gentle boys.

"How dare you speak to me in that tone of voice? Who do you think you are?" I told him after our guests left.

"I think I'm me, and I'll talk to you any way I want," he shouted, undermining my interpretations of history. Furious and wounded, I reached up to push his muscular shoulder. He knocked my arm away and yelled, "Don't put your fucking hands on me!"

Later, we argued for an hour about whether he had said, Don't put your fucking hands on me, as I remembered, or, Don't put your hands on me, as he insisted. Finally, I gave up. "Oh, just forget it, but don't ever say fucking to me again. I'm your mother."

"How can you say that? You say fucking all the time!" His voice a screech, losing almost all the new, low tones.

"I say fucking about things, not to people," I answered.

"What's the difference between saying, Turn that fucking music down, and saying, Get your fucking hands off me, which I never said?" We were chin to chin, but I was losing control of the argument.

"You don't say fucking anything to a person's face, directed at them. You use it in the third person."

He raised his eyebrows at my distinctions and returned to the subject of why he had been what I called fresh and he called just angry.

"When I'm angry at you I have to talk to you in a harsh way, or even scream, Mom," he told me, lying down on the bed that only two years ago had been much too long

156

for him. "How do you expect me to sound when I'm angry? You spoke to me in a mean way first."

By this time I could not confidently remember who had spoken harshly first to the other. Perhaps I had embarrassed him in front of the guests, and to save his pride he had to be fresh in return. I recall the pride of my fifteen-year-old self, mortified before my father's public chastisements, my cheeks heating to purple flame. My whole story fell into doubt, and I was left with the warning that I am his mother, and you should be especially careful how you talk to your mother in public, but here I was reduced to the future conditional and only a declarative certainty would warrant punishing him. My authority threatened to become mere melodrama, an empty, pathetic tyranny.

The last time I'd punished him for freshness was when we all went with Daniel to the doctor. "I don't want to make any promises," Dr. McVale told us. "But the diabetes could remain in this easily controlled stage indefinitely."

During the detailed explanation of his brother's prognosis, Anthony began playing with a scale. Metal bars clanged. Measuring rods whizzed up and down. "Anthony," I said. "Please!" But he continued, creating a percussion of metallic background noise to our possibly regenerated hope.

A year before, we'd all stood in the same office, still as heat, listening to the words of the diagnosis roll toward us like summer thunder. Daniel's face was a small boy's again, eyes wide at the shock of injustice. Then I saw him blink, an awful recognition aged him, and in that instant his childish innocence was gone. When I returned from the bathroom where I'd rushed to vomit, I tried to pay exquisite attention to the numerous details of care we now had to manage. I hovered over his shoulder, trying to gain control by imagining my story in the third person. But Daniel, an excellent reader, can gauge my mood accurately by the rhythm of my breath or the pitch of my murmuring. "Mom!" he shouted, and I walked out of the tiny office to the laboratory next door, up and down the aisles between rows of vials and bottles, Bunsen burners and scales, files and faucets.

Dr. McVale, a gentle, childless man, said, "You have to let him go now. You would have had to anyway, since he's going to college. Now more than ever though."

I picture myself holding Daniel in my arms as I walk through the rooms of our apartment. He is only a few months old, and I cover his tiny bald head, where the fontanel still beats vulnerably, with my open palm to protect him from corners and walls I have a tendency to bump into. When I put my hand on his head that way, I believe I am obliterating some boundary between us, as if throughout his tiny body he can feel the power of my vow to protect him from the world and from the limits of myself. Whatever power I possess, he can rely on, and since that power still seems limitless when I am twenty-five, so do the dimensions of his reliance. I picture myself holding Daniel in my arms, and then I try to picture opening my arms gracefully, turning away. "You just have to let him go," Dr. McVale repeats in a firm whisper.

There is a rope swing over the deep part of a beautiful lake I visited with Anthony. He grabs the rope from his perch on a high rock and swings in a wide, swift arc over the water. Back and forth, gathering momentum, and while he is over the rocks I am struck dumb with fear, for if he should let go at the wrong moment, his bony frame will shatter. But he does not let go, nor do any of the other brave teenagers. At the widest point of the arc, at just the right moment, safely over glistening water, they let go and fall into the lake.

"You don't let go of a child the way you let go of a rope," I tell Dr. McVale, humbly and without rancor.

In the next few weeks, Daniel's fingers will become sore from drawing blood, the soft flesh around his belly black and blue from repeated injections. You can only take a shot where you have fat, but Daniel has thick thighs, developed triceps, sinewy forearms. A strong boy who could always take care of himself. Anthony, everyone thought, was the vulnerable one. But it was Daniel whose footsteps I waited for coming down the hall, Daniel's accidents and falls that seemed potentially emblematic, Daniel I lost in my dreams. I try to let go of him as he masters new controls on which his life now depends, yet ancient words come from my mother's mouth without intention, repetitive warnings, terrible clichés. "If you want to know the truth," he finally says, "I feel pretty strange having you know my blood sugar level at all."

"Have you had your snack?" I will ask, mastering new recipes, preparing food with the attention I had once used to measure formula or add fresh fruit to a previously all-cereal diet. "When will you be home?" I cannot refrain from asking as he leaves for his summer job in a restaurant. Once when he is fifteen minutes late, I will call the manager, who thinks Daniel is a college graduate and living alone, and trying to make my voice sound young ask for my son. When I hear his voice I hang up without saying hello, as one might calling a former lover in the middle of the night.

"Come to my house in the country, and get some rest. Leave him alone," Joanie calls to say. "He needs me," I insist. "He doesn't need you," she tells me brutally. And so I am on the bus to Springfield, and outside my streaked window Interstate 95 moves past like thick steam, the houses and trees losing clarity and outline until it's all the same undistinguished gray. He will be better off alone with his father, I tell myself. I am giving him the best thing I can, the absence of the persistent anxiety he hates. There was a colorful chart in Dr. McVale's office illustrating genetic patterns and possible causes. Virus. Autoimmunity. Recessive gene. Stress. The last word devours the rest of the color-coded design and goes neon, for who has caused him more stress than I? But now I will let him go gracefully, legs bent perfectly, arms outstretched, face pointed to the sky, and I will surface smiling, as you do, Anthony, easing into a slow, restful crawl. When we left him standing in front of his new dorm, his medical attentions habitual after three months of practice, his stereo, saxophone, new sweaters and down quilt, family photographs, books, desk supplies, piled up in his tiny room waiting for his arranging, I turned my back after an elegantly restrained embrace. It was dark by then, and Bruce and I had a four-hour drive ahead of us. Suddenly Daniel was grabbing us from behind, pulling us together in his arms, murmuring a blessing on our parenting. I hope he turned and fled quickly enough to miss the sound that came from my throat, some prehistoric creature's unintelligible squawk, far beneath language.

"I have never seen a boy your age maintain such perfect control," Dr. McVale was saying to Daniel when Anthony's scale playing got so loud that I had to shout at him to stop so we could hear the doctor talk. He was so rude to me that when we got home I grounded him for three weeks. He didn't cry at all, just stared at me with cold black eyes that remained stony from Friday to Sunday. I cried continually, as if I were in mourning, although I had every reason, now, to be hopeful about Daniel. I was sitting at my kitchen table with my head in my hands, weeping, when Anthony touched my fingers and said, "Why do you keep crying, Mom?"

I fell into his lanky arms. I told him how I hated it when he spoke to me disrespectfully. "What will the doctor think? That I can't even control my own child?" I said.

"Well, how do you think I feel in front of Dr. McVale, when you shout at me to stop playing with the scale as if I were a baby?"

"Then why were you playing with the scale like a baby when we were trying to talk about Daniel? You made me nervous, Anthony."

"You could have said it nicely," he repeated, and took his hand from me.

So I dropped the punishment after only one grounded Saturday night, and I realized why I had been crying all those days. When they were small, I counted on the miraculous fact that they would always forgive unjust discipline, an unintended wounding, even plain unkindness. They'd waddle after me, begging for reconciliation. Now it is I who cannot bear to have them mad at me. This is not the way to appear consistent and controlled to one's adolescent children. Good maternal practice requires conviction. How are they supposed to be clear about limits if the mother keeps muddying up the line?

Now that Daniel's gone to college, I amaze myself with peaceful, sleep-filled nights. I thought I would wake regularly, wondering where he was in a strange city, wandering down unfamiliar streets. Who would even know if he failed to return to the dorm? They don't have curfews anymore. But as soon as he was on his own, I relinquished all hope. I had practiced for two years, from the first September day he became a high school junior. Next year is his last, I said to myself as soon as he swaggered out to school, and I planned a program of slow discipline. When he was in cars, driven by new young men just born from driver's ed., I imagined the worst. If they crash, there's nothing I can do, I'd intone, allowing resignation to replace anxiety. Resignation is an emotion I can live with. It invokes the bitter comfort of realism, a knowledge that I am seeing clearly. I fear anxiety more. While that blinding storm rages, I keep thinking I should be doing something, provide protection. Some neglected vigilance will be the cause of ruin—batten down the hatches, tape the windows. And the mirrors! Pack the mirrors in quilts. There is nothing I can do, I will whisper, lying in bed waiting for him those last minutes before the clock strikes curfew, two A.M.

"Why not set the clock for five after two?" Bruce asks in his most annoyingly objective tone. "Then you can avoid anxiety. He's almost always in on time. By the time you wake up he'll be home."

But in those ten minutes before I hear his key in the door, I must regress to old forms of magic. I picture him getting a cab on a street corner, still light and crowded with people despite the late hour. Or he is sitting safely seat-belted in his most reliable friend's car, and the friend has had nothing to drink since he is the driver. Or he is walking down the safest streets, since Daniel is street-wise after all these years. I picture him physically to enhance his unarguable strengths. Daniel is six feet tall, broad-shouldered, slim-hipped, square-jawed. Still, "What if he gets mugged?" I once asked Anthony when Daniel walked away from us on a dark street. "Mom," Anthony reminds me grimly, "Daniel's the one people are afraid is going to mug them." I fear the police too, Daniel looks a little tough. "Button your shirt up," I whisper to him in the dark. "Tie your sneakers. Don't run on the street, especially on Park Avenue."

When it is ten minutes to curfew I invoke the last-ditch magic of the not yet rationally resigned. I picture him tall, careful, safe. If an image of danger intrudes, I cut it like an editor trimming a story. Focus, I tell my writing students, focus is your glue, your momentum, your art. I pile up images, trying to teach them a desire for precision, the ecstasy of total control. I focus on Daniel, keeping the story trim, a safe story about a reliable boy who puts his seat belt on when he sits in the front. At two on the dot, at most two minutes after, Daniel walks in. And I pretend to be asleep when he touches my hair to let me know he's home. Good night, my darling boy, I often find myself saying, however, a too passionate endearment for the middle of an ordinary night. As if he had escaped the government police in Johannesburg. As if he had returned from the front, the son of a Nicaraguan mother. And what will I do if he has to go to war? I often asked myself before drifting off to sleep the whole year he turned eighteen. On an ordinary night I might have said, good night Daniel, or even good night honey. On the night of his diagnosis I said good night my darling boy, and I went to my bed in the ruin of a storm whose aftermath of resignation and sorrow was so far beyond the discomfort of anxiety, I longed all night for the illusion that there was something I could do. My heart beat its regular, idiotic rhythm, and my pancreas went on cruelly making insulin as his was no longer able to do.

In the beginning there were no words. In the beginning was the sound, and they all knew what that sound sounded like.
— Toni Morrison, Beloved

Maybe she ought to stop here, but fragments of stories pile up. She can never remember them all. She will suddenly recall perfectly unintentional translations made by her children when they were young, their early attempts to make sense of the world. She wishes she had a code, a computer design that could call up the detailed records of memory without her feeding it all in first.

Once, when Anthony was about four, he threw his arms around her and Bruce, pulling their heads together, and, imitating her, he crooned, "My boys."

Soon after Daniel had begun to identify himself as "interracial," Anthony, then about six, had said, "Daniel thinks of himself as being Jewish. You know how he's always saying he's into Rachel"—referring to a close friend who had recently converted to Judaism.

One night, when he was in the first months of kindergarten, Daniel told her he was confused by school. "Like today," he said, brows raised, hands spread apart in perplexity, "all day we kept singing, Happy Birthday, Martha Lutha King. Who is that lady?"

All the brilliant confoundings of language and meaning spin in her head tonight, recalling a child's world of undecoded fictions. "Once upon a time," Daniel mut-

tered to himself over and over that year he entered the city's educational bureaucracy, "Daniel went to school." Each evening another chapter emerged in the third person, the narrator gaining increasing control.

She will lose many of these stories. It is not enough to take notes, a scrapbook of memories. But she has to stop somewhere, refocus her attention. Tonight, she sits at the oak table, her notebooks opened before her, recovering from the intensity of the street.

Tonight it is raining hard and turning cold. On my way home from a restaurant where I've been having dinner with a friend, I am stopped by a young homeless woman who is obviously freezing. She wears no hat, and her long kinky hair stands up around her head, dripping water onto her forehead, into her eyes. A tan raincoat only partially covers her small body. Her dirty white blouse, buttons missing, is opened at the neck, and her chest is wet from the driving rain. She holds on to my arm and says, "I need food. Please give me money for food." She does not seem at all inured to life on the streets but is as desperate as I would be in her place. I pull my arm free to search my bag for my wallet. "Please," the woman shouts. "Give me something!"

"I'm going to give you something," I say. "I'm just looking for some money."

As if I haven't spoken, the woman grabs my arm again, shouting, "Please!"

Nearly shouting myself now, I tell her, "I am! I'm getting it!" I find my wallet, pull out a five-dollar bill, thrust the money into her hand, saying. "Here. Take it. There's a Chicken 'n' Ribs right across the street."

I begin to walk away, but she is calling after me, "This isn't enough! I need more!" Maybe Anthony would think I should have given more.

I look behind me after going another block, ready to turn around if she is waiting, but she is gone. Perhaps she has only taken temporary shelter in the supermarket or the vegetable stand and will emerge any moment, pursuing me. I am beginning to feel cold and wet beneath my heavy coat, isolated and endangered on the crowded street. Panic is building with every step I take. I concentrate, conjuring up my home. Bruce and Anthony are probably watching a late Knicks game, or Anthony is still doing homework and Bruce is reading the papers on the living room couch. I will kiss them both, change into a flannel nightgown, read myself to sleep. But it is too late. I am falling into a narrow fault in the earth where I see Daniel's skin pierced by too many needles, as close to my eyes as the woman who is gone now but whose terrified face has taken its place in my mind. Divisions break down, and all I can do is write to regain equilibrium.

She continues writing, although precise transitions elude her. One thing leads to another without warning. She imagines a linear narrative, a plot, but it is a fantasy; she knows she'll never feel the ease of such a story again. Memories collide. Threads of years.

In the long network of hallways on the eighteenth floor of the hospital where Daniel was first diagnosed, Bruce was a familiar specter, walking so slowly that at times I put my palm on his back, afraid he would stop still, slump downward from lack of momentum. As we followed our daily schedule from nurse-practitioner to doctor to nutritionist, he could not stop crying. Every so often he embraced Daniel or held his long fingers, murmuring, *Sugar,* his old pet name, which had now assumed an ironic twist. Daniel received his father's ministrations graciously. It was me with whom he was often furious. "It's because you're the one he's most dependent on, and now he's forced to an independence that awes even Daniel," my friends told me. It is because he is still angry at me from the early years, I thought. "It's because you're so anxious you can't remember the simplest things, which makes it hard for me," Daniel said. More than ever before in my maternal life I try to be what I am not: confident, optimistic, self-forgiving, radiating a promise of security and faith. I shut my thoughts away, watching him closely when he measures insulin into the hypodermic, when he deftly pierces his flesh. "Don't stare at me," he says. "Don't you think I'm strong enough to do it on my own?"

Eventually Bruce returned to himself, but there is a crack in the armor so that even years later I hesitate to show him these pages. "I'm afraid you'll start crying and not be able to stop again," I say. But after he reads them he says, "No, I feel good. You made Daniel seem so strong." I am trying to refrain from thinking about him every minute, to resist imagining every possible story. But then Anthony decides to do a report on diabetes for his science project, and I cannot seem to read the books he bought although that was my original intention. Instead, I cannot stop thinking about a rolled-up drawing I brought to a framer recently. I asked that it be "floated" as the artist had instructed, but it had remained rolled up too long and would have to be matted, the framer said, because "paper remembers." I remember folding up, remaining silent. I remember relinquishing something, the exquisite relief.

All these years I believed my childhood was behind me, and I suppose it is, but now images are hauled up on the shore of my consciousness like grotesque fish, flesh bloody, torn by hooks and teeth of sharks yet pulsating, refusing to die. Some nights my mother walks the floor again, disease killing her slowly, week by week for three years, eating her flesh until there is almost nothing of it left. You are not Daniel, I tell her. This is another time. These are two different stories.

She died too young to annoy me with maternal attentions carried on beyond my need for them, too young for her worst character flaws to become my own, to seem the stone against which I had to carve the shape of my identity. It would be left to me to assume that ordinary maternal destiny, and I would feel toward myself as many people feel toward their mothers—shocked at every impotence, enraged at every failure, contemptuous and unforgiving. One night Daniel called me from college, his first year. He had seen a film from the 1940s about a mother and daughter parted all their lives. "I'm so upset by that movie, and I don't know why," he told me, and then, breaking into tears, "All my life I have been haunted by your mother."

I will never completely forget the image of her body, the feel of her bones. At times I suddenly remember the sensation of Daniel's legs against me when I carried him, knees pushed gently into my waist, heels patting against my thighs as I walk clumsily, my back aching from the weight of him but the flatness of his cheek against my cheek so comforting I don't want to put him down. I remember with perfect specificity the contour of Anthony's neck, which was thicker than Daniel's, the tiny pointed cyst behind his ear, the high curve of the arch of Daniel's foot, two darkened marks at the base of his spine. I always knew these bodies were ordinary, like any others poignant in their combination of awkwardness and grace. It was their ordinariness that suggested an idea of perfection.

When she concentrates most fully she feels solid and grounded. Her mind feels lucid and thoughts move slowly, effortlessly gaining language, like a wagon wheel gathering mud into the grooves of its tread. It is not that she is a woman or not a woman when she writes, but that she is safely inside herself, a dark place, almost black, filled with voices and images that are clear, then disappear again.

When I was a child I had hallucinations I called "the feelings." The first was the "crayon feeling," in which a sense of my body contours disappeared until there was no clear outline of myself, as if I were inside a huge crayon, hiding within a blimp-shaped thing. Then I would begin to write or draw until I felt ordinary again. There was the "finger feeling," which used to send me rushing to my father until he rubbed those grotesquely ballooned fingers into normality again. Now, when that feeling comes, I know I am missing someone, even feeling the eventual loss of someone who may still be around, keeping the airy bulk of them in my hands. And the "suitcase feeling" was the last. My arms begin to ache weirdly from shoulder to wrist, they feel almost paralyzed, as if I have been carrying heavy suitcases too long. This is guilt or anger at being unequal to the tasks imposed on me, tasks such as bringing the dead to life with my voice.

When she was a child, she had two voices. One learned to say what was expected and possessed the body that was not quite hers. The other voice was interesting and personal but had no sound and no place. She began writing to repossess her body. She remembers her amazement at the first movement of her children inside her—the turning over, a shifting as unmistakable as wind. Inside her body—hers—what had not existed before existed now. So she understood that one day she would cease to exist— her flesh certainly, and most likely her consciousness, too. She has no certain faith in any sort of immortality. Rather, she begins slowly but regularly to imagine dying so she can prepare. She discovers that just beyond the fear lies some extraordinary sympathy she can only call love, and this sympathy extends even as far as herself.

If the spirits of the dead are with us I can feel them, I sometimes think, but the bodies are what I want—the sound of a woman's breathing, boys calling me before their voices changed. In my obsessive search for convergence, I risk a permeability that can sometimes be dangerous—I know this. Walls collapse like sand. The pit of the crazy women opens within me. I hear Bruce's old question: Why are you all like this? We are hungry for symmetry, for some rare collusion between the world's reflection of us and our knowledge of ourselves. The emptiness in that breach is bottomless. I rummage through piles of food, devouring things—bread, chocolate. I drink juice, wine. Afterward, knowing I ought to run or walk at least, I go to bed instead and fall into instant sleep, smiling, satiated, dreaming of children's lives perfectly repaired, books perfectly read.

Once when she wrote she felt she was pushing herself into the world, demanding with every new word that someone listen. Now, she contracts. She remembers her inner organs pushing upward when she was pregnant, giving increasing room to the baby. When she writes now she feels like that, increasing the space around her, making a place for something new. Now that she has nearly finished these stories Julia feels a mixture of fullness and hunger. By putting herself in the third person she somehow cheats the shaming, and she is free to retain and explore her own point of view. Yet, attached to this freedom is a new constraint, a form of silence increasingly familiar to her with Daniel and Anthony.

When Daniel was three years old and I was pregnant with Anthony, he asked me where babies come from. When I explained, he asked if I did that with his daddy. We were walking in our neighborhood, hand in hand, and I said, "Yes, to make you." "Then I want to do it with you too," he said.

"No, you can't," I answered. "Children don't do that with their mothers." Up to now we were an ordinary mother and child, generic.

But Daniel began to scream at me: "I want to!" He shouted so loud, people turned to look at us as we passed.

"You can't," I whispered, teeth clenched.

"Why?! Tell me why!" he demanded. "If Daddy can do it why can't I?!"

I failed to calm him down or shut him up but dragged him screaming across the street. Now we are no longer just anyone, we are Daniel and Julia, two people with the virtue or fault of undeveloped boundaries, too much passion for normal standards of social life. But sixteen years later, he is sitting near me, reading. He has been depressed for the three weeks of a summer visit and has just told me in quick summary why this has been so. "I feel strange," I say, "not knowing much about what's happening in your life. You can be sad or upset and I have no idea why."

"Let's face it," he tells me, distant and manly, "you'll never know as much about me or my life as you used to know."

Lately, Anthony has begun to withdraw into his hereditary silence for reasons unknown to me. He shuts the door to his room as soon as he enters the house, emerging only for dinner, then again to say goodnight. I keep my distance, practiced now in the harsher aspects of the discipline of motherly love. A second child, he does not incur so heavily the burdens of history, and I feel sorrow more than anger. One night, I am awakened by a hand stroking my face, a head lying heavily on my shoulder from the wrong side of the bed. It's a tired mother's nightmare, I think at first, some stranger breaking into my room to steal nurturance. Just before I am about to scream, I realize it's Anthony.

"Don't ever leave me, Mom," he whispers into my neck. But his words can be understood only if inverted, for why should I leave him? I would beg him with his own words, lie here forever with the weight of his head causing my shoulder to ache. I would preserve the precise feel of this ache, add it to my store of hallucinatory sensations. I can feel the time, five or ten years from now, when I may need it, when even the memory will have dimmed and some other woman will hold him in the dark.

"I won't leave you," I say. "Of course not. I promise."

She will write what she sees outside her window, what Anthony said to her the other day, her dreams. If nothing else, she will write what she would like to write tomorrow. But so much resists explication. Beneath the truth of words is another reality, more definitive and brilliant and in some dangerous way more easily known.

172

—I was crazy when I was a child, I once told my children.

—Oh, come on, Mom, said Anthony.

—No, I mean it.

—Like what? Like you heard voices or something? (His tone sarcastic.)

—Yes, as a matter of fact I did.

—Oh, my God. Dad. Is she lying?

—No, I don't think so.

—What kinds of voices?

—Old ladies cackling. People I knew. And my own, as if it didn't belong to me.

—Oh, that's just your imagination, says Daniel. And you know yourself, Mom, your imagination is always running away with you.

These boys had a far saner childhood than I did. They do not understand that feeling crazy is not always some monstrous, otherworldly state but can be simply a wild unfamiliarity with what others consider to be ordinary life. An inability to live unselfconsciously. A tendency to find miraculous the fact that Bruce hangs up his suit, puts on his sweat pants, sits down to read his paper without a voice in his head saying: He hangs up his suit, he puts on his sweat pants, he sits down to read his paper.

Julia is a character I can only imagine, a portrait of a woman who has the courage to write a portrait of a woman who writes. I wish I had her bravery, or Daniel's. She has been some sort of deliverance for me, with a definition I lack, a focus I can manage only occasionally, an ability to endure losses and survive. She can go back into the white silence at a moment's notice. The world does not compel her to explanation or revelation as it once did. Perhaps it never will again. But inside, in the space as black as the dark heart of Armstrong's blues, there are messages, ideas, lyrics, poems. She longs to hear them clearly. And the price (now it is a price) is the discovery of a pattern of language through which someone else might understand. When she was young, her voice was a liberation. Now it is a burden—perhaps futile, or sacred—the perfect construction of a sentence.

She sits down at the oak table and opens a notebook. Anthony is going out for the evening, and the weather has been frigid. "Take a hat, Anthony," she calls as he waves to her from the doorway. She knows he won't, it will mess up his hair, and knowing she knows this, he zips his parka up to his nose, smiling tolerantly. Daniel would have gotten angry at her pointless persistence. Yet she had never been able to stop, to recognize this son's need for daily autonomy, not until he was too old to care. If she had the chance to do it over, she would do it differently, she thinks, the sound of her own voice in her head a chorus explaining centuries of parental flaws. "Be home on time," she chants, knowing she needn't say this to Anthony. "One-thirty." He steps out the door. So she rises and opens it again, calling down the hallway, "Okay?" Then he capitulates. "Okay." And he is gone.

"I can do without this," I say out loud, confronting the notebook. I am a woman who writes and a woman who does not write. My words will not control the world, not bring the dead to life, not even change the fate of my own flesh. There is more to reality than language. Maybe people will read my words a hundred years from now. Maybe all those pages will disappear along with a million soda cans and plastic packages. At first it doesn't seem to matter, not compared, for instance, to my certainty that Anthony will come home on time. In the next instant words are magical again, the only hope I have.

I pick up my pen and hear another echoing chant. *She would write these stories differently if she were to begin again.* Sitting at the table, the house quiet now except for the hum of my thinking (Bruce is in his room reading; Daniel has returned to school after a long vacation in which everyone tried to avoid combat and we had managed three weeks without a single fight—until one evening Anthony spoke rudely to Bruce, then I interfered, then Daniel jumped in, criticizing me for intruding on fights not my own), I recall the feeling of foundations crumbling, then the surge of power and contentment as day after day I found the most precise words to describe the shifting, shaky movement that had become my life. Why should this be so? The words did not quiet the shaking, only provided some containment, an outline that does not alter but identifies a shape. Without the words there is a blunted, unchallenged vision that, I see now, I have relinquished, or escaped, again.

She cannot feel detached, transcendently separate from the children, ever again impervious to human flesh. I write this down, calmed by the only perspective I know. I am aware of some new energy I cannot yet define. Desire wakens me in the night, comes upon me in a crowded room. I imagine the delicate pressure of hands on my body. The flesh of someone else is scintillating. I take swift notes, feel as if I can read people's minds. Then desire fades again, and all the patterns I see are conventional.

I am afraid of being born into this new life where I have no children to force me out of blind immanence into the troubling world of their experience, where my sanctuary lies in increasing consciousness and nowhere else. They have drawn me with designs of hidden and obvious images, and I see everything more clearly through their eyes. Twice, recently, I dreamed of hardened clay roads inside my body. They are turning to dark, rich mud and there, sculpted with half-visible patterns, is that old wooden wheel, vines of black leaves and purple spices twisted into its spokes. They are the vines that grew wild in my mouth and throat when my voice was worn out and insufficient. They were tangled around the tombstone over my mother's grave and pushed through the casement window where I heard my grandmother's song. The wheel moves slowly. At first it makes no noise and the white air around it is still. Soon, I hear a low humming as it gathers layers of mud. Then I am as black and blue as Bruce, or Daniel, or Anthony. I am black inside where loss, language, and courage will root for as long as I live.

Movement, patterns. And silence.